Leading the Dance

Sarah Salway

Published by bluechrome publishing 2006

2 4 6 8 10 9 7 5 3 1

First published in Great Britain in 2006 by
bluechrome publishing
PO Box 109,
Portishead, Bristol. BS20 7ZJ

www.bluechrome.co.uk

A CIP catalogue record for this book is available from the British Library.

ISBN 978-1-904781-88-2

Printed and bound in Great Britain by Biddles Ltd., King's Lynn, Norfolk

Acknowledgements

'Bodily Fluids', 'Family Tree', 'Quiet Hour', 'Painting the Family Pet' and 'Jesus and the Aubergines' first appeared on eastoftheweb; 'Painting the Family Pet' in *Shorts*, ed Candia McWilliam (Edinburgh: Polygon, 2001); 'A Lovely Evening' on pulp.net; 'Chains' in Product magazine; 'Blind' and 'The Woman Downstairs' in Quality Women's Fiction magazine; 'Maggots in the Rice' in *Pool 2*, ed Tobias Hill (Wirral: Headland Publications, 2003); 'The End of the Ice Age' in London Magazine, and as prizewinner for Writers Inc 2005; 'Toad in the Hole' in Buzzwords magazine; 'Leading the Dance' in *Teaching a Chicken to Swim*, ed Rob Middlehurst (Cardiff: Seren 2000)

Contents

Chains

Sunday morning. You go for the paper. Walking head down
through the park, you worry over too-early daffodils and curse
dog owners but what you're really thinking about is how just ten
minutes ago your wife whispered that she'd never come like that
before, and how she told you that whoever said sex got boring
hadn't met you. When you hand over the money in the newspaper shop, you're automatic in your agreement that, yes, you too
throw half of it away a load of bloody advertising; but all the
time you keep hearing that little gasp your wife gave, the one
you can't remember her making before, a little cry that exploded
into your neck, so childlike, so trusting, and you're puzzled because all you did was make love just like you've always made
love. You were even a little bored until she gave that cry. And as
you retrace your steps what should give you so much pleasure
starts to gnaw at you so when you stop and prod a chain on the
ground with the toe of your shoe, you're only half aware of picking it up and putting it in your pocket but as you walk on, you
get to like its heaviness, the clink clunk of the links jiggling
against each other and you put your hand there and joggle some
more like your granddad used to do with his loose change. You
do it a couple of times and it makes you feel old and solid just
like him, so when you see the dog come towards you, the woman
chasing after it calling its name - *Freddy, Freddy* - you don't veer
off like you normally do but you swoop down and catch the dog
by its collar and hold it saying there's a good dog, and trying to

soothe it like you would a child. And when the woman comes up and thanks you, tells you that the dog's lead broke and then the dog ran off and crossed a busy road, you pull your hand out of your pocket and put the chain on the dog, snap, like a lover fastening a gold necklace and it's with the same feeling of pride that you hand the dog back. A gift. But the woman's looking at you oddly now, perhaps she's wondering why you've got that chain, so you just back off and walk home with the newspaper, and when you go into the bedroom your wife raises her head just slightly from the pillow and says I'm too far gone to move, come back to bed, and you're tempted but then you think of that gasp. You say you're too busy. She comes into the kitchen later and kisses the top of your head and you feel her open gown pressed up against your back but you shrug her off and say for god's sake can you think of nothing else and then you have to leave because you can't bear how hurt she is although it's her that's in the wrong, it's her that always wants more than you can give, and you can't walk through the park again in case you meet the dog woman so you go into town instead and look into shop windows at all the things you would never want to buy.

Friday comes and it's a relief to go out because even dinner party conversations are preferable to being at home. Every time your wife opens her mouth you realise you're waiting for that gasp, the little intake of breath that fills your head. At the party you tell a story against yourself, you say how you picked up a chain in the park without thinking and how good it felt in your pocket. Round the table everyone laughs so you embroider slightly. You say the woman had screamed when you came towards her with the chain and that the dog had leapt up but you'd calmed it down and there's something so warm about having a table of friends wonder at how a person like you could be taken for an attacker that you smile at your wife who's sitting there, watching you. She smiles back and you mouth the word *later* and she closes her eyes just slightly the way that makes your guts jump so filled with lust is it, that hooded blink. You drink the rest of your wine and think that maybe everything will be alright now and when you excuse yourself and go up the stairs you half expect the shadow waiting round the corner to be your wife but it's the woman your best friend brought with him and you've already noticed how she won't stop looking at you. You say pardon me because she's blocking your way and she whispers something into your ear that you can't quite make out so you just smile and say anything back, a comment about the food, the evening, your best friend, and it's only later, when you're in bed with your wife and she's lying with her back towards you that you realise what this woman said. She said that she likes chains too. And now you can't stop laughing. It bubbles out of you with the shock of it. You're thinking of your best friend and how he'd always run away from anything like that before. It's one of the many things you used to share and now suddenly you wonder when the sharing stopped. Then you imagine him with the woman and you see him clearly, trussed up like a Christmas turkey, and all of a sudden you stop laughing and although your wife has turned away again, you can tell she's not asleep, her shoulders are tensed up and she's built a wall with them, pulling the sheet taut against her. Your fists clench and unclench on top of the covers and she tells you to stop grinding your teeth and you turn to her and say. You say nothing because all you want to say is stop.

For weeks you avoid your friend but when he finally rings, you rush to the phone.

He pretends he doesn't know who you mean when you ask about the woman and when you say that he must, he brought her to the bloody party, you can hear the hesitation in his voice and you know he's never going to tell you. You're surprised at how angry this makes you so you finish the conversation quickly although you wanted to meet up with him. He's still the only person you can ask whether it's possible for women to learn new noises because your wife's made it again and she clawed your back too, just slightly but in a way she's never done before and it's driving you crazy although the sex is good, it's never been better and you can't get enough, you're never out of bed these days. And you want to tell your friend this but you know he doesn't want to hear. His voice is all tight, clipped, he says the woman was just someone he'd met, that she was nothing serious, you say well in that case you'd like her telephone number, there was something you were discussing with her you'd like to follow up. And then he asks how you are and you say fine just fine. No, nothing's wrong. And then you think of your wife and you say is there any reason why I shouldn't be fine and he laughs. You don't sound it, he says and you are just about to tell him everything but then you remember that split second at the dinner table, sitting next to him, when you looked at your wife and you thought maybe, just maybe. What you don't have to think about again is what the woman said to you because you relive it all the time, the way she stopped you on the stairs that night but these days you hear every syllable the woman says. You hear the words again and again and it seems to be everyone that's saying it. Everyone but you. Even when you manage to get some sleep, your wife comes to you in your dreams and she makes that little sigh too and once you thought she whispered your friend's name and you weren't able to tell her to stop. You think about this as you put down the phone and fold the telephone number your friend has given you into your pocket, so when your wife asks about your friend you have to leave the house and as you walk away what you think is what if, what if.

And the next time you walk through the park, you don't look down, and when you go into the newspaper shop it's to ask for the paper to be delivered although you used to like the Sunday morning walk, and when you walk into town you don't bother to look in the windows because you know where you're going and although it's embarrassing you don't think twice. You're sur-

prised at how many people are in the shop, you had no idea.
When the man wraps the hand-cuffs you don't make any conversation although you want to, you want to ask whether many
people buy these, you want to find out what you've been missing
out on. You want to fill the gaps. You leave the shop and walk
back across the park. You don't catch anyone's eye. You're
thinking of your friend and the woman he brought to the party
who stopped you on the stairs. And you're thinking of your wife.
And when you put your hand in your pocket to feel your parcel,
it doesn't jingle and you don't get any pleasure from the cold
steel, but you carry on walking. You thrust your hand deeper
into the pocket, clutching at the hand-cuffs because you can't
stop thinking about that gasp.

Painting the Family Pet

A strange woman comes to my door one day in early March. It's a prosperous area so we often have people selling things door-to-door - dusters, make-up, frozen foods - but she doesn't look like a professional saleswoman. She hasn't got the patter either. She just smiles awkwardly and thrusts a card in my hand: 'Amy Turner. Pet Portraits Undertaken.'

I run my fingernail along the cheap gold edge of the card and look at her, waiting for an explanation.

"I'll paint any animal in the comfort of your own home," Amy Turner says. "Wouldn't you like a unique portrait of your loved one? I've had experience of dogs, cats, parrots, prize bulls..."

"Prize bulls!" I can't help looking up and down our suburban street. The thought of any of my neighbours keeping bulls in their back gardens makes me smile but then I see that Amy looks cross and I realise I've interrupted her sales pitch.

"I don't have any animals," I say as we look past each other. She must be wishing some little cat or dog would come running down the hall to give the game away and it's the first chance I've had to sniff the air outside. It is one of those spring mornings when you wake up and find winter's gone. Even the camellia in the garden opposite has flowered overnight, vulgar pink blossoms which look shocking against the quiet greens and greys.

"Why are you still in your dressing gown?" Amy says, turning her attention back to me. "It's nearly lunchtime. Are you ill?"

"I'm fine," I lie. I'm not going to tell a stranger I've just been sick in the toilet upstairs and would still be sticking my fingers down my throat if the doorbell hadn't rung. But now I'm not sure what to do next. Amy is still standing there. She doesn't seem to think that not having a pet is a good enough excuse.

"I'm starving," she says and I smile politely, nodding the way you do before you say goodbye.

"No," she puts her foot in the door. "I'm really starving. I've had nothing to eat for two days and no-one has any sodding pets for me to paint. I need some food or I'll faint, right here on your doorstep."

I move to one side and let her in.

Amy stands by the fridge playing with my poetry magnets while I make her a chocolate spread sandwich. I brush past her to get the butter but really I want to see what she has written.

> WOMAN RUBS
> SILKY SLOWLY
> PINK BUBBLES GLOW
> COOL HEART
> BLUELY MUSIC

I used to write proper poems to Dan once upon a time. When we were first married, I would tape them to the fridge door on scraps torn out of a spiral bound notebook. But then he bought me this expensive set of magnetic words and I couldn't write any more. Even my poetry had turned into something only he had the power to give me. I play with the words in their little glass box sometimes but I've lost confidence in my ability to use them in the proper sequence. I'm disappointed that Amy isn't even trying to make sense.

"Aren't you eating?" she asks as she nibbles round the edge of the sandwich. She is so delicate, her tongue curling upwards to lick the crumbs off her upper lip. If she'd really been starving, wouldn't she have crammed the whole thing in at once?

I go to the fridge and open the door, pretending I'm looking for something so I don't have to answer her question. I can feel her come up behind me but I stay there, memorising the names of all the food as if I'm about to take an exam.

"Do you always keep such a lot of food?" Amy asks.

"Do you always ask so many questions?" I say quickly, but Amy just laughs. She's standing so close I can smell the chocolate on her breath.

"I could paint that," she says, pointing at the fridge. It's one of these tall American models. I dream about it sometimes, a huge monster standing in the corner of the room with its mouth constantly open and I'm this tiny little figure, exhausting myself in my efforts to keep it satisfied.

"Why would I want a picture of a fridge?" I ask.

"Because you seem to like looking inside it." Amy shrugs and goes back to her sandwich.

"But I can just do that, can't I?" I persist. "It's not like an animal or something that could die or get old or change."

"I could paint the door of the fridge with what's inside. Exactly as it is now." Amy sounds as if she's explaining something to a slightly dim child. "Then you won't need to keep opening it and wasting electricity."

There are so many reasons why this doesn't make sense that I look at Amy standing in my kitchen and I don't have the energy to argue.

"I'll start tomorrow," Amy says, studying her fingernails before she starts to gnaw at a cuticle with more enthusiasm than she showed the sandwich.

When Dan comes home, he goes straight to the fridge.

"Good day, Helen?" he asks, slurping from the can and wiping off the moisture from his top lip. He stands in the kitchen doorway, staring at me.

He does this all the time. I've learnt not to mind, although recently he's taken to creeping up on me so I don't know how long he's been there. It's not too bad during the day but I find it hard to go to sleep at night, knowing he'll be looking. I prefer it when I've time to arrange myself, like now, legs underneath me, skirt fanning round my body, arms resting on the back of the sofa, gaze averted.

I nod, but I can't help wondering if he messed up the fridge when he got his beer.

"Whatdayadotoday?" Dan comes to sit down next to me, and I can feel his weight upset the balance of the sofa. This is how he talks, so fast that all the words run into one. He does everything on the gallop; always has done. "Dan needs to slow down and look at the finer details of his life," his primary teacher said in her report one year. It's a comment Dan wants to frame and stick up on the toilet wall.

"I'm thinking of getting a pet," I say, folding my body under the arm he's holding out behind me.

"A pet." Dan pretends to be shocked, but then he sees I'm serious. "No, baby, you don't want to do that. Animals take up too much of your time."

"It would give us something to talk about," I say.

"We talk enough," says Dan. "I'm not coming home tired from work and discussing what the hamster's been up to."

"No pets then?"

"No pets."

We eat out, although I know Dan's seen how much food there is in the house. Dan orders rare steak for both of us and after he's finished his, he leans over and spears the half of mine that's left with his fork. A drop of blood falls on the white tablecloth, about three inches away from the vase of plastic yellow flowers that sits between us.

"No point in wasting good food," he says, and I excuse myself to be sick in the ladies. To waste good food.

Dan watches me make my way back to the table, past the thick wooden bar counter and the fake palm trees. He's fingering the bill that sits in the shallow bronze bowl in front of him. Dan's not a mean man, but I wonder if he's thinking the same as me. Do you have to pay for food that doesn't actually leave the premises?

The next morning I wake up feeling excited, not sure why. I wonder what I've been dreaming about and then I remember Amy. And then I remember Dan. Dan eats breakfast. I rush downstairs, barefoot, to check the fridge. If he's finished the milk, it could spoil the picture.

I lie down on the sofa so I can watch Amy paint. It's taking longer than she thought because she has to keep opening the door to check on the proportions.

"Why don't you buy one of those Polaroid cameras?" I ask. "Then you could just paint from the pictures."

"Do you think I'd be doing this if I could afford a camera?" she says.

I don't even listen to the words because I suddenly realise something. Amy answers every question with another question. The fact that I can anticipate Amy's behaviour pleases me. She is no longer a stranger.

Because Amy's in the kitchen anyway, she makes us both coffee every time she needs a break. She brings over the two steaming mugs and sits next to me on the sofa.

"So if I wasn't here, what would you be doing?" she says.

It's like a test. I wonder if there is a right answer she'd like me to say but then give up.

"I'd probably just be sitting here," I say.

Amy shakes her head. She fizzes with so much energy that I'm scared to touch her in case I get a shock. I like it when she sits next to me because we balance each other out. I can feel her body physically relax as her aura meets mine in the middle. It's different with Dan because his energy takes over until I'm colonised, diminished. Amy is more unfocused so mine beats hers every time.

Two hours later, I start to notice that Amy is looking at the clock almost as often as me.

"It's lunchtime," she says blandly.

"So it is," I say, handing over the decision to her.

"We'll spoil the picture if we eat anything from the fridge." She runs her fingers through her short red hair, looking worried. "Shall I nip out and get something from the shop?" Amy's already putting her jacket on so I stay still. I've wrapped the duvet round me now, my head just popping out at the top.

"Surprise me," I shout as the door shuts behind her so softly I know she's left the snib up so as not to disturb me.

"Did you look at my painting?" Amy asks when she comes back and I shake my head. "You've not moved all morning," she says. "Not many people can keep that still. Animals, now. That's a different story."

She hands me first a spoon and then a small glass jar.

"Baby food!" I hold it in my hand as if it's a precious object, and whisper my thanks so quietly I'm not sure Amy hears. However, she slips in when I hold the end of the duvet up for her to get under and we spoon smooth organic carrots into our mouths like two baby birds in our feathered nest. I can feel the puree worm its way down my throat.

"I knew I was right about you." She looks triumphant as she holds out her hand for my dirty jar and spoon.

When Dan comes back that night, I say nothing as he heads for the fridge.

"So what's going on?" he asks, coming straight back into the sitting room. It takes me a moment to realise what's different about him and then I realise he's not got a drink in his hand.

"I'm having the fridge painted," I say and he comes over to give me a hug, holding me so tight that I feel the breath forcibly expelled through my mouth.

"My wife, the one and only Helen," he says as if he's announcing me to a room of strangers. "No one else but you would do this."

"It wasn't my idea," I say quickly, but he's back in the kitchen, shaking his head and staring at the fridge. From his smile, I suspect that he's already thinking of the story he'll tell the people at work the next morning. "Just guess what Helen's done now..."

We go back to the same restaurant and I tell him about Amy while he eats both steaks. I embroider wildly on all the stories she's told me that day and he laughs so much that he doesn't notice I'm not eating anything. This time, he pays the bill straight away and we leave hand-in-hand.

Amy and I experiment with our lunches. She prefers the leek and potato puree while I move towards country parsnip. The day before she finishes the painting, we celebrate with a fruits of the forest dessert, taking it in turns to dip our spoons into the jar.

"What will you do when you finish here?" I ask.

"I'm not fussy. I'll paint anything so long as I get paid," she says, looking at me oddly. "Will you miss me?"

"I'll have your painting to remember you by." I try to think what I could give Amy, but she seems to move through life without the need for possessions. Dan's sorting out the payment anyway. They've started to have coffee together in the mornings before I get out of bed. I can hear their laughter come up the stairs, curling under the bedroom door like a tendril of smoke. I'm pleased Dan has someone to let his energy off onto. He's got so bouncy from all the steak he's been eating.

Dan and I are positively vivacious as the waiter shows us to our normal table. I tell him which animal I think Amy prefers to paint - cats - and he says I'm wrong. She likes dogs best. We talk about Amy all evening and when we let ourselves back into the house, we're still laughing.

"Whisky?" Dan asks and goes to get the Laphroaig. I stand in the kitchen and stare at the fridge door. Amy is a real artist. The chicken breasts look as if you could reach out and pick them up, she's even got the little crumbs of toast Dan always leaves in the butter and the curl on the yoghurt lid is exactly right.

"It's better than I thought it would be," Dan says, handing me a glass. I swirl the liquid round and round the glass, pressing my nose in as if I can taste the peat better that way.

"Will you buy me a camera to give Amy?" I ask. "Then she won't have to spend such a long time in other people's houses. She can do the painting at home."

"I think living in other people's houses is what Amy likes," Dan says. And then he laughs so loudly that I'm forced to give in and ask him what's funny.

As Dan reaches into the cupboard and pulls out the picture, I remember Amy's words about how she would paint anything if she got paid. She's flattered me. My hair's not as long or as thick as she's made it and there's something attractive about the wistful way I'm looking just slightly off the canvas.

"It's a joke," Dan says, when I don't laugh

I know it is. It's Dan's joke. The one he always makes when people ask me what I do. He tells them he stops me from doing anything because he finds me so restful to look at. "In the same way some people keep a goldfish to calm them down," he says.

He must have told Amy this because she's painted me swimming round a glass bowl. I hold the picture closer to my eyes to try and make out if the shadow at one side is another person or not. I guess I'm hoping Amy's painted herself in the water with me.

Dan must be aware he's gone too far this time. "It's nothing personal," he says. "Amy's not like you. She has to earn her own bread and butter. Come on, Helen, we've all got to eat."

After Dan goes to bed, I draw up a chair and sit in front of the fridge for a long time. Then I spend some time opening and shutting the door. Amy's painting is like a piece of tracing paper laid over the real thing. She's even managed to get the light just right. I stand in front of the open fridge as if I'm warming myself and turn round to look at the spot where I normally sit and keep her company.

I start with the yoghurts and then move on to the cheese, cutting it up into small pieces. While the chicken and bacon are cooking, I tear up lettuce leaves and hold them above my lips as if I'm sucking on peeled grapes. The butter I force down in one, washing it through with two pints of milk. I find some chocolate at the back and eat one chunk after each raw egg as a reward. Every ten minutes, I open one of Dan's beers and toast the distorted face I see in the bowl of the spoon I'm using as my weapon. I save the ice cubes until last, biting and crunching them between my teeth until I can feel the ice splinter and crack. I open my mouth and icicles fall round me onto the floor.

When the fridge is empty, I let the door swing shut and lean up against the painted front for support. Then, slowly and deliberately feeling my way with both hands, I reach into the cupboard under the sink and bring out the bundle of supermarket bags I keep there. I fill each one with good food and leave them in as straight a line as I can manage for Amy and Dan to find in the morning.

The End of the Ice Age

If he tilts his head just slightly to the side, he doesn't have to see the plastic orange glow of the hotel gas fire. He can just feel the heat on his skin and pretend it's logs burning.

He shuts his eyes, feels the pressure points of her body leaning into his bare skin. He used to make snow angels every winter when he was a kid. Like them, he thinks her weight will leave the imprint of dips and curves on his surface until he becomes a mould she can pour herself into.

"I'm too heavy," she whispers into his ear. "I have to go to the airport soon anyway. I really can't miss the plane." A fall of her hair tickles his cheek, so he moves his mouth to catch it, his nose burrowing to find its faint musky scent. He pulls at a strand with his teeth and watches her wince.

When she tries to slide off him, he catches her by the hips, his palms resting on the hollows he finds, his fingers pressing into her flesh.

"Stay," he says.

"Forever?" she asks. "We'll be found here in six months time, our skeletons locked into one. Just think. They won't be able to tell your shinbone from my arm, your tibia from my femur. At least they'll have to bury us together."

When she flops over to lie by his side, he raises himself onto his elbow and traces a line from her hip up the curve of her belly, spreading his fingers to cup her breast and then moving sideways to circle her arm. She lies so passively that, when he leans across to kiss her, he thrusts his tongue fiercely into her mouth at first before feeling along the edge of each tooth. Then when he's finished, he licks the outline of her lips with the tip of his tongue so gently she starts to smile involuntarily and he pulls her to him, nuzzling his head in the curve of her neck.

"We wouldn't decay that much," he says.

"How do you know?" she asks. "We *could* end up a pile of old bones."

"Think about it. If we lay in front of the gas fire for that long, we'd cook. Hordes of folk would come knocking at the door enticed by the lovely meaty whiffs. They'd think we'd opened a restaurant."

"Eat me," she says, but when he bends his head down past her belly, she laughs, pushing him up.

"Not yet," she says. "Tell me a story first. But make it a quick one. We don't have much time."

He's about to say if she's in so much of a hurry, why should he bother, but just then her legs fall open so that one thigh rests against his, skin on skin, and she takes his hand and puts it between her legs. He lets it lie still for a few seconds and then he starts to rub backwards and forwards with his palm.

"Where do you want to go to?" he asks.

"The wood, always the wood." Her eyes are shut, her head falls on his shoulder.

"OK." He pauses a moment to picture the cabin, imagines catching sight of it from the path and walking up the three wooden planks that make the steps to the deck. He will pause a bit to look over the open view. Once inside, he'll light the wood-burning stove first and then strike matches to the candles, shake out the rolled-up mattress on the floor, take cushions from the kitchen chairs and lay them out on the ground. When everything looks fine, he'll open the bottle of wine and pour himself a glass, before crouching down in front of the fire to watch the logs start to burn. When he sees a shadow pass the mirror they've set up to warn for strangers, he'll open the door.

"I'll pull you inside quickly and kiss you and kiss you," he says. "I'll pick up a blanket and wrap you up in it, I'll rub you through the wool until your skin start to crackle with the static. I'll breathe on your neck to warm you up, I'll..."

"Wouldn't we be wearing any clothes? I'm not sure I'm up to streaking through the countryside. You forget it's cold in England this time of the year." She turns over so her back is spooned up against his side. He slides his leg under hers. His hand plays with her breast, squeezing and teasing her nipple.

"I suppose you could have a coat," he says. "An ankle length herringbone coat, but you're not to wear anything underneath it."

"It has to have a purple silk lining," she says. "I'd like to drive to you like that, feeling the silk roll over my body."

He slaps at her naked bottom, before leaning over and placing a kiss on the red mark. He traces the length of her spine up and down like that, before coming back to lick the small of her back. He can feel that she's stopped breathing. That she's waiting to see what he'll do next. He leans away from her and she pushes back into him, so he can tell how much she wants him.

"I'd pour you some wine to cool your wicked thoughts down," he says. "We'll sit in front of the fire on the mattress and you can tell me about your journey."

"It was a long and difficult one so I'd be hungry," she says. "What would we eat?"

Ah, he hadn't thought of that. Still, he can tell she guesses she's got him there. Probably thinks that this means she can start to take over the story. He thinks quickly. "I'll put my hand in the pocket of your coat," he says, "and pull out a packet of boiled sweets. Pear drops. Remember the smell of pear drops?"

"I used to suck them until all the sugar came off," she says. "Then I'd roll the smooth ball round and round in my mouth."

He strokes her skin all the time as he thinks about this. He can't stop touching her, playing with her. The gas fire really does become the log burning stove; the cheap foreign hotel room is a cabin in the wilds of the countryside; the wind at the window is whistling through trees, not electricity cables. They have all the time in the world, not just an hour left in a day that's been stolen from the rest of their lives. But he wants to take a break from the story now and ask her about sweets she enjoyed in childhood, whether she remembers sherbet fountains, liquorice wheels, candy shrimps and those Black Jack and Fruit salad chews you got for four a penny. It's the ordinary things he wants to know.

He pulls her to him, holding her so tightly he doesn't think he's ever going to be able to let her go. He tries to remember back to where they were. Her voice when it comes is shallow and tight.

"Would we just eat the sweets?" she asks.

"I'd dip one in my glass of wine and leave snail trails over your body," he says, pulling her onto her front and hoisting himself on top of her. He's still not inside her yet, although his cock is nudging at her legs, trying to find its way in.

"I'd be sticky," she laughs, and he pushes the tip of his nose round her ear.

"I'd lick you clean," he says. "I'd cover every inch of your body with my tongue - inside your elbows, behind your knees. I'd find my way into every secret part of your body. All the places nobody else has been before."

"And when you've painted me with pear drops, what would we do then?"

"I'd put the sweet up you like this," he says, thrusting two fingers inside her, and then he opens her up wide and comes into her finally. He kisses away her sigh. "And then I'd go down on you and try to find it. I'd lick you and lick you so I could taste your sourness against the sickly sugar. I'd pull it out with my teeth and push it back in with my tongue. I'd feast on you."

He moves as slowly as he can bear. They're clumsy with each other, it's one of the things he loves about her. Still likely to elbow the other, or go the wrong way in the duet. Now though she holds on to his back tightly to keep him close and he can feel each outspread finger against his skin, the way the nails dig in slightly. He bends his head down to kiss her arm. The small goosebumps on her skin graze against his lips. He stops, still inside her, and just holds her. Lets her hold him.

"Oh god, I love you darling," he says. He starts to move again and when he feels her tense, he's pleased because he thinks she must be about to come, early for her. He grabs her arms, wants to make this last as long as he can, but she's fumbling on the ground by her clothes. He rolls off when he sees she's searching for her watch.

"You'd better go," he says flatly.

She sighs. "I'm sorry. Please. We've got time," she says.

"No, not like this. Too cold and calculating." And when he looks at her again, he can't picture the wood again. All he can think about is how he feels when she goes. The loneliness of that period between leaving her and going back home. How quickly the assurance that what they're doing is right and clean and the only way to be evaporates into a sick thud at the bottom of his stomach. How the disappointment sullies everything he touches. How he promises himself that this will be the last time, that this time he can survive without her, and how this thought sustains him, strengthens him until he almost believes it, almost convinces himself that he doesn't want to even hear her voice again.

She pulls him to her. "I'm sorry," she whispers. "Please go on. What noises can we hear in the wood?"

He pushes her hand off him. He turns his head from her kisses. "The sound of your plane taking off," he says, and regrets it the minute he sees her curl away from him.

They both lie there without talking, but then she moves her head round so she can see him. He loves the curve of her back. The way she looks at him just like this when she wakes up on the few nights they've slept together. But this is different.

"I'll go," she says and he watches her scoop up her clothes and hold them over her body as she walks to the bathroom to get changed. He lies there on the floor, playing hide and seek with his clothes. A sock here, his pants there, a shirt over the chair. He just looks at them, leaves them lying there.

When she comes into the room again, she's fully dressed, her hair's pinned up. She starts to rummage around her handbag and pulls out her make up bag.

"So when will we speak again?" he says. He doesn't know why he's not making the effort to even get up from the floor. Is it to deliberately annoy her?

"Let's just leave it, shall we?" she says, pausing in what she's doing for a moment to look at him through the mirror, the mascara wand frozen in mid-air.

"OK." He's surprised at how light he feels. It's as if snow has thawed from all round his body. He feels as if he's finally been released from the block of ice that has held him captive for the last two years. If only he'd known before how little it really took. He still doesn't move from the floor, not even when she leans over to look at him.

"Really?" she asks, and he suddenly sees that she wants to stop too. The heat in the room is almost unbearable. He feels he is melting away, like the cartoon snowman who sits too near the fire. He wants to touch her, just to see if she is evaporating too. Maybe they'll disappear into a pool of liquid, which the maids will mop up in the morning. He reaches up and at that moment she falls back down into him. He pulls down her tights, her pants, quickly, pushing his fist harshly between her legs. She's so hot there. He wants to warm his hands on her fire.

"No," he says. "Not really."

And he turns her over so he's on top of her. He unbuttons her shirt, lifts up her skirt and comes into her like that, with no stories, no wood cabins or frosty mornings. They move together in a plait that only they can untangle and when they look into each other's eyes they see just the one thing. Home. They're so gentle and tender and slow that the tension is almost unbearable and when they do come they sink into the other even more closely, as if what they want is to dissolve into the other's flesh. This is every answer they've ever wanted. This is why there'll never be any going back. This is their reality.

Later when he waves her off at the airport, he stands for a while, watching the closed departure door. He thrusts his hands deeper into his pockets and plays with the frayed fabric of the seam edges. The slippery surface of a single wrapped boiled sweet twists through his fingers. He tastes her sourness still on his lips and if he raises his nails to his nose, he can smell the dustiness of dried juices there.

As he drives along the autobahn, he thinks of the wood cabin. When he looks out of the window, he sees not the mountains but the view of the rolling hop fields. What he remembers is the taste of the white wine licked from her back, not the lukewarm cup of tea they really shared.

And as he gets nearer to his house, he begins to notice how the countryside is changing. He remembers the magic painting annuals he used to get every Christmas and how one of his favourite things was painting the blank pictures with water and seeing the colours emerge out of nothing.

But now when he looks at the too familiar scenes from his car window, and thinks of her sitting up there in the clouds on the aeroplane that's flying away from him, he watches the colours of his own life dissolve into plain white paper once again.

Paper as white and as unmarked as ice.

Quiet Hour

Malcolm has to stay very, very still. He is sitting on the stone lion on the front porch. He is part of the lion. He is a statue.

Sometimes he will forget and itch his leg or wipe his nose with the back of his hand but as soon as anyone walks by the house, he'll snap back to attention. Only his eyes will move to see whether he has been noticed or not.

It's a hot afternoon. The sun feels prickly on his arms and through his thin cotton T-shirt and shorts, he can feel the warmth over his whole body. It's on days like this he'll choose to sit on the lion. He likes the feeling of the smooth stone cool against his legs.

Malcolm knows nearly all of the people who could pass by, but he's waiting for one in particular. If Malcolm's truthful, this man is normally the only one he sees. He knows why. It is quiet hour. For an hour after lunch, you have to be very quiet and restful if you want to grow big and strong. That's why it is important for little boys, although it is Malcolm's mother who is asleep upstairs on the big double bed. Malcolm knows that quiet hour is over when his mother comes down and then he can make as much noise as he likes, although it is never as much as his brother and sister make when they come back from school.

There are only a few things Malcolm likes to do on his own. He prefers to play with his mother, singing songs and telling stories. It was his mother who had the idea of the statue game, which is funny because she isn't normally good at making up games. Sometimes, Malcolm can persuade his mother to walk up and down the street in front of the house, saying "that's a nice statue. I'd like a statue of a little boy on a lion just like that." Malcolm will sit very still then. He won't even move his eyes.

He hasn't told anyone else about the lion. His brother and sister would tease him and although he doesn't mind when Susanne laughs, he knows Jonathon would have played once, before he went to school. Malcolm is going to school after the summer holidays. He's got the uniform already, and the pencil case filled with coloured crayons he is only allowed to use to practise writing his name.

When he hears the car crunch up the gravel drive, Malcolm is so surprised he forgets he is a statue and runs across the grass, hobbling over the pebbles in his bare feet.

His father is sitting in a white car he hasn't seen before. Malcolm isn't sure which is shiniest - the car or his father's face. He gets out and shuts the door very carefully so Malcolm can hear the clunk.

"Where's Mum?" his father asks after he has lifted Malcolm up and whirled him round the way Malcolm loves. The buckle on his father's belt is digging into Malcolm's leg so he moves it quickly, kicking his father so hard he is dropped on the gravel.

"We mustn't wake her up. It's quiet hour," Malcolm explains, examining his knees for cuts.

"She'll want to see this," his father says. "This is our new car."

Malcolm smiles at him and says it's a nice car because his father is looking as happy as he felt when he got his new yo-yo with the glow in the dark string.

He holds his father's hand as they walk together up the stairs, although Malcolm stays behind when they go into the bedroom in case his mother is as angry as she was the time Malcolm woke her up to tell her about the big ginger cat that had come into the garden.

From the doorway, he can see his father bend over his mother's sleeping body and whisper something in her ear. Malcolm doesn't know what it is but his mother sits up sharply, as if she's had a nasty shock. But then she looks nearly as excited as Malcolm's father and this makes the butterflies dance in Malcolm's tummy too. A new car!

He copies his mother as they walk around the car, not just once, but twice, three times. "It's lovely," they murmur as they run their hands all over the shiny surface.

"Shall we go for a ride?" his father asks and Malcolm is surprised when his mother says yes. He can't remember ever going anywhere with both his mother and his father on a school day.

The leather seats are as hot on Malcolm's legs as the lion was cold. Malcolm squirms around until he finds that if he keeps his legs still for a little while and then lifts them up, it sounds as if he has farted.

"Stop it, Malcolm," his mother says from the front but she doesn't sound cross. Malcolm does it again, but this time he looks under to where his leg was on the seat. It is all wet with the sweat, with little bubbly bits where the edge of his shorts were. Carefully, he wipes away the marks with the sleeve of his T-shirt, and then pulls his shorts down, sitting on the edge of the seat so that no skin touches the leather. He has to keep his bottom still, but manages to lean forward so he can put his head between his mother and father to hear what they are saying.

"It's a beautiful ride, George," his mother is saying. "Really comfortable."

Malcolm's father puffs out his chest. He starts to point out all the things on the dashboard - a clock, buttons to press when it's dark or raining or if you have an accident. Malcolm likes this red one best. He stretches over to press it but his mother shouts at him.

"What's that one?" he asks, pointing instead to a large round button.

"It's a cigarette lighter," his father says, pushing it in. It stays there for a few seconds and then pops out, surprising Malcolm. His father shows Malcolm the orange swirl in the middle but won't let him touch it.

"Really lovely," his mother says again, and Malcolm's father smiles, putting his hand in front of Malcolm and on to his mother's leg. He keeps it there so Malcolm sits back and looks out of the window. All the buildings and trees are going by so quickly, he doesn't have time to see where they are.

"Slow down, George," says his mother but Malcolm's father just laughs and seems to go even faster. Malcolm can see he is holding really tight onto his mother's leg now.

Malcolm sits very straight as they go back down their street, hoping that someone will see him in the new car. If they do, he will wave like the Royal family does on the news.

When they pull into the drive, he expects them to walk around the car again but Malcolm's father is whispering to his mother. Malcolm can see his mother frown, but then nod.

"It's still quiet hour, Malcolm," his father says. "Mummy and I are going to have a little sleep before the others come back."

Malcolm doesn't want to sit on the lion again. He knows how cross Jonathon will be that he was the first to ride in the car.

"Can I just stay here?" he asks, and his father opens the car door quickly for him whispering that he's to remember not to wake his Mum, that earlier on was a special occasion.

At first he stays where he is, practising waving out of the window but it isn't much fun when there is no-one there so he climbs over to his mother's seat and leans across. "A lovely ride, George," he says when he suddenly has a better idea.

Now, he is the one in the driver's seat. Brum, brum. He can feel the bubbles of spit gather in the corner of his mouth when he makes this noise. He sways from side to side as he pretends to take the car round a sharp bend, and then the next one. He's going very fast, and no one is telling him to slow down. All of a sudden he comes to a stop. He's won the race and everyone is cheering. He turns round until he's smiled and waved out of every window. Thank you, thank you.

To begin with, Malcolm doesn't notice the man standing in the driveway watching him but when he does, he sits up straight. A statue once more.

The man smiles at Malcolm. They've played this game before.

"Well, well," he says. "They've got a new statue. It's a little boy driving a smart new car. Isn't that grand?"

Malcolm likes the way the man says grand. It makes him want to laugh but he doesn't. He stays motionless, looking out of the front window, although from the corner of his eye, he can see the man making his way up the path to the side door.

Malcolm's mother has explained that all sorts of people need quiet hours. Sometimes people live too far away to go home so they have to visit other people's houses and share their quiet hours. "Like sharing your toys," Malcolm asked and his mother laughed and said it was something like that.

Malcolm thinks it's funny that men need quiet hours. His brother doesn't and he won't next year at school. Still, his father is upstairs now, so perhaps he goes to some other Mummy's house normally. On the days he doesn't get a new car.

Suddenly, although he doesn't know why, Malcolm doesn't want the statue man to go into the house.

He tries to open the car door but he can't find the handle so he pulls again and again until something gives way. It's just the ashtray. He bangs on the front window, trying to get the man's attention but it's too late.

Never mind, he thinks, the others will be home soon so maybe they'll all go for another ride then. He'll show Jonathon where everything is, waving his hand over the dashboard, copying his father. For practise, he presses in the cigarette lighter, counting until he can hear it pop... One potato, two potato, three potato, four... Malcolm pulls it out and swishes it around the car as if it's a magic wand, glowing at the end with fairy dust.

The first time he presses the hot end of the lighter against the dashboard, it makes a funny noise - pheewow - like an explosion of air. He likes the way the black leather puffs up all around the edge of the lighter and the complete white circle that's left when he pulls it away.

But when he tries it again, the circle's lines are fuzzy, like his paintings when they smudge. He tries another one - even smudgier - before clicking the lighter in its hole again and shutting his eyes tight, counting. Now he wastes no time. He knows it has to be as hot as it can get. It's like the potato print patterns he does at nursery but better because there he's only allowed to use paper.

He's just finished decorating the dashboard and is about to start on the roof, when he sees the man coming out of the house, followed by his mother and then his father. They're all shouting so it must be the end of quiet hour, but although he sits up straight and doesn't turn his head to watch them go, no one seems to notice what a really good statue Malcolm is making this time.

Toad in the Hole

It was lying under the hedge when we found it. Jamie saw it first.

"If you want to be in our gang, you have to pick that up," he told Mikey.

I still don't know how a toad's biology works but the insides of this one were hanging by a thread from its mouth like a red cartoon speech bubble. We stood in a circle round the body and took glances up at Mikey. He was going to cry soon, so half of us looked back down at the toad while the other half studied Mikey closely so as to be first to see the tears.

"Well go on then," said Simon. "Pick it up."

Simon was an ideal number two. What he lacked in brains he made up for with a cruel streak that needed to be fed regularly.

"It's not fair. I've done all the challenges," Mikey said. He had, and more. But no one had applied to join our gang for a long time now, and if we didn't hold elaborate initiation ceremonies then there was nothing else for us to do.

"It's in the rules," said Jamie and we all nodded. You didn't argue with the rules.

Mikey leant forward, his face white, and Steve prodded me. "He's going to touch it," he whispered.

"Gross." I forgot to keep my voice down. Jamie looked over.

"And you..." Jamie pointed at me. "You have to lick it."

Steve took one step away from me. Matt did the same on the other side. I ignored Mikey's look of sympathy. I hated him. This was all his fault.

For the rest of that term, boys went ribbit, ribbit, every time I came near them. No one wanted to be the friend of the toad licker. I got so sad that my mother kept taking me to the doctor to check I was all right.

"He has no energy," she whispered as if I didn't know this myself. The doctor felt all my limbs, listened to my chest with a cold stethoscope and said I was a growing boy and needed more food to fatten myself up.

My mother kept cooking me toad in the hole.

No, she didn't. But it would have made a better story if she had. I learnt a lot about good stories, and lying, and saying the right thing over that time. I learnt to laugh at myself in order to survive.

In biology, the captain of rugby threw up all over the desk the day we did hearts while a wimpish boy called Kevin took his cut-up heart home in a Safeway's bag, boiled it and ate it for his tea. He started a trend. When it was time to dissect frogs, everyone jostled me all the way into the lab and said yum, yum. I tried to laugh it off but then Jamie told Simon to toss the frog over to me so it would land on my mouth.

"Stick your tongue out, toad licker, there's a treat on its way," he shouted but Simon did not have a good aim. We all watched, our mouths shut firmly but unable to move, as the frog sailed through the air in slow motion, its legs and arms perfectly suspended like a kite until splat it landed on the window only inches away from Maryanne Franks and stuck there while we all held our breath. Then slowly, it started to slip down the glass, leaving a red smear behind it. Maryanne screamed so loudly she had to be taken home. Everyone else got to draw the reproductive cycle of the frog for the rest of the afternoon. Jamie turned his picture of tadpoles into sperm and Simon laughed so hard that Ribena came out of his nose.

I am a vegetarian these days. If anyone asks me about it, I tell them I do it for economic reasons. If I throw in enough statistics, it shuts people up. Occasionally I meet a smart alec who tells me that Hitler was a vegetarian and it always makes me think of Simon. I wish I could tell you that he is a vet now, or runs a pet shop, but he is a fitter in a local factory. Jamie is an accountant and drives a blue Jaguar. When we meet up, we shake hands and say ribbit, ribbit and laugh a lot. I could cope with this better if I felt more confident that Jamie could remember why we do it. He introduced me the other day as his oldest friend and I really think he meant it.

Me, I married Maryanne. We have the cleanest windows in town.

Every Time You Open Your Eyes

It's funny the way you look at things these days. You used to tell him how you loved those little grunts of contentment he made in his sleep. Now you just long to shake him awake to stop him dreaming about her.

> *Do you love me?*
> *You know I do.*

You know I do. She knows he does. And now you also know he does because you've found the letters, the postcards, the e-mails printed off so as to leave no record on the computer, but too precious for him to erase completely.

It's a medium designed for lovers. A quick, heated touch that can't be taken back. A snatched interlude from real life. Without reason, without forethought, without foundation.

> *Do you want me?*
> *It's only ever you.*
> *Do you miss me?*
> *More than I can bear.*

You check the date. He wrote that on the day you took the children swimming together. He laughed so much when Robbie did a belly flop that you dived over to kiss him. To hold him close so you could catch his joy too and spread it round for everyone else. You could afford to be generous then.

> *More than I can bear.*

42

It would be hard to believe if you hadn't seen it. And there's more. You've made yourself read them all. A poem reminding them both of a moment special only because you haven't shared it; a children's joke you find to your horror you're smiling at before you catch yourself; angry words from an argument half-given, half-understood and then the make up.

> *I'm sorry.*
> *No, I'm sorry.*
> *We're stupid.*
> *I should kiss you, stupid.*
> *Spoiling our summer.*
> *Our lovely summer.*

It's all so trivial. Innocent enough for you to want to read on until you realise why you're doing it. She's taken him back to the man you fell in love with. The man he used to be before the family started to weigh so heavily on his shoulders. You'd forgotten what he was like. What you both were like. You're so hungry to keep remembering that only sometimes does the truth hit you.

> *Do you wake up in the morning and wish I was there?*
> *Every time I open my eyes.*

Every time he opens his eyes. Every time he opens his eyes he wishes she was there. That you weren't. Watching him sleep now, you lie still, not breathing. Taking up so little space in the bed that used to be your sanctuary. Do you...do you? Of course he does.

You talk to him about it. Scream, weep, try to find reasons. It was love, he says. Pity, you reply, if it was sex I could have understood. He looks interested then. Really, he asks, sex is better? You think, not for the first time, that men are different from women. He seems to think that it is less of a betrayal to love someone than to fuck them.

He takes your hand. The one that secretly sifts through the envelopes and white paper to follow the trail he leaves. You feel pleased then that you haven't told him about finding the box where he keeps her letters. It's all over now, he promises. I see how foolish I've been. How much I've put at risk. It's you I've loved all along.

That night you have sex rather than make love. I'm making an effort, he says later, and you say nothing. You don't even tell him that you've just read the letter. The one she sent that morning saying how she understands he has to be more careful but what matters is their love for each other. Nothing can destroy that. Just look at how much we've come through, she says.

Searching through the papers you at last find his reply. The e-mail you always knew would be there because remember, once, a long time ago, you used to know this man.

You are my own true love, he tells her. *You are fine, and good, and honourable. My heart is breaking.*

The next morning he goes to work late so he can make you breakfast in bed. He puts a rose close to your face so you can smell the garden you planted together once upon a time and then he anoints your forehead with a drop of dew he's found on the petals. Like a christening, you say. Like a beginning, he promises.

Where are you? Her e-mail demands that afternoon. *I've been ringing you all morning.*

Busy, he replies. And then, one full heartbeat later. *Busy missing you.*

I am making an effort, he repeats weeks later and again you say nothing. Even if you hadn't read his letters, his sadness would tell you the truth.

I can't bear to cause more pain. His words jerk out like sobs. *The destruction would be terrible.*

Only if you don't create something in its place, she writes. *Something more honest for everyone involved.*

I can't. I can't.

And he can't. You always knew he could never do anything like that on his own. That's why it hurts to open the box. You stay in bed each night after he falls asleep wondering if today it will be worth it. If this will be the day she persuades him to reveal the man you always hoped was still hidden there. The one who opened his eyes joyfully in the morning. The one you miss as much as she does these days.

We have to be strong, he writes. *We have to do the right thing.*

Do you love her? she asks and there's a new hesitancy in her question. She's lost the easy confidence that attracted even you and you feel the sadness like a stone in your stomach.

There's love and love, he says.

You sit there staring at the paper, resisting the urge to go through to the bedroom and wake him up. It's as much for her sake as yours that you want to know what this means.

You search through the box for her reply, but there's none. The letters are carefully folded, so you take them out and check the dates. You think you must be wrong. But you're not.

There's love and love.
The end.

How could she leave it like that? To let so much pain close with a meaningless line. Is this what you've put yourself through hell for? You feel cheated, angry with them both for letting you down like this. You close the box heavily, slip back between the now cold sheets and stare at his sleeping profile, trying to force your own particular brand of love to fill up the space that's growing between you.

*

It's months later and you tell yourself that if he says he's trying once more, you'll leave. You're looking for excuses these days. In an attempt to bring some cheer back between you, you tell him something funny the kids have done but he looks at you blankly and it hits you that so much of what has gone on between you has had value only when it is something he can repeat to her.

Do you love me? you ask him one evening when you find yourself alone together.

You know I do, he replies and you hold him tight so you can pretend this love is enough. That this is what you both are looking for.

Later on that night, you go back to the box, blowing the dust off the cover so the fingerprints won't show. You take out the last piece of paper, turn on the computer and as the lines of text flicker over the screen, you search for her address. Your heart is pounding and your fingers are electric over the keyboard as you start to type.

I was wrong, you write. *There's only one love that really matters. Talk to me.*

It's not hard to sign his name, and then just one button to press and it's gone. Out of your hands. Out of your control.

The next morning, you wake early so you can watch him open his eyes.

Good morning, you say, and for the first time in a long, long time you mean it.

Bodily Fluids
(after Hélène Cixous)

To Travel Hopelessly

Dave's waiting to cross the road, shuffling from one foot to the other in his impatience, when the woman next to him suddenly puts her hand on his arm.

"Excuse me," she says. "I really am terribly sorry to trouble you, but I think I'm going to cry."

A merciful act of rescue is not always seen that way by everyone

She does cry, both in the street and in the ladies of the small cafe he takes her to. As he waits for her, he spoons the froth from the top of his cappuccino and see-saws the sugar in the little paper envelope, as he tries not to listen to the wailing coming from the toilet. She can't have known how thin the walls are. Behind the counter, the blonde waitress stares at him in open contempt, banging cups down hard on the metal counter every time he looks in her direction.

The woman smiles at him, though, when she finally emerges. Apart from a slight red bruising under her eyes, you wouldn't have been able to tell what she's been doing. Her mouth is a slash of red and he's surprisingly moved to see a lip-stick smudge on her front tooth.

"Your coffee's probably cold," he says. He wants to ask what went wrong, but it seems too intimate. And probably, more truthfully, he doesn't want to be caught in the middle of something he suspects might be messy.

"You must think I'm mad," she says. "I can't really blame you. I've never done anything like this before."

"Well, I can't say it happens to me often," Dave says, pulling his wallet from his jeans pocket, "but if you're feeling better I'll get on."

"Please let me get this. It's the least I can do." He takes note of her gold watch, Rayban sunglasses, expensively tailored black jacket and decides that yes, buying a cheap cup of coffee is a pretty small gesture of gratitude.

A Romantic Entanglement

"But what do you think was the matter with her?"

Eleanor is sitting astride his chest, facing his cock which she's kneading between her palms. She's looking over her shoulder at him as she talks and he'd appreciate a little more concentration on the job in hand. She has the tendency to be rough at the best of times.

"She was a bit old for it to be a love thing," he says. "Maybe she'd had a bad day at work, her parents had died, I don't know. What do people cry about?"

"You said she was in her late thirties."

"So?"

"Could have been love still. Maybe she's unhappily married but has an all-consuming passion for a Russian violinist. He loves her back, but can't give up hope of finding the wife he'd married when they were teenagers. This wife refused to come to England when he defected and they've lost contact. He's just

told this woman that without a divorce they can never be together."

"Eleanor ..."

"What? It could happen. You've no romance in your
soul, Dave."

"No, it's just that you're hurting me."

She drops his penis so it slaps on his stomach and he
thinks he's done it now, she'll be storming off in one of her tan-
trums, but she edges her way down his naked body. He can feel
the brush of her pubic hair on his skin before she impales herself
on him.

He's aware of how unsexy it feels, dry almost. As if Eleanor's too businesslike for body fluids. As she works on top of
him, he remembers the tears running down the woman's face as
she asked for his help, wishes more than anything that he'd
thought to mop them up. Even licked them away. The image of
his tongue lapping at her cheek gives him a jolt, causing him to
buck up, nearly unseating Eleanor.

"Steady boy. I know you love this but I'm not ready
yet," she calls and he can't help noticing her voice captures the
rhythm of her up-and-down movements. With each breath
taken, her buttocks slap against his stomach. Dave tries to picture himself back with the woman, sheltering her under his arm
like a wounded bird. He's just drawing her to him, hushing her,
settling her sobbing body when Eleanor starts to scream. He
winces as she hits his sides, whipping him on. He struggles to
match her frenzy. If he hesitates, causes Eleanor to lose her
pace, she'll be really angry. He's only done it once. Never again.
Eleanor says he's lucky enough to be given a second chance as it
is.

Leaving bad habits behind for good

He'd met Eleanor in the university library. He knew of her, of course. Everyone did. Not many Americans came to study at their provincial university, especially not one who had already started publishing in academic journals, given papers at conference, was even rumoured to have a book contract in the pipeline.

She was smaller than he expected – probably only about 5ft 1in - but stocky. Her red curly hair was clipped short but she was constantly playing with it, raking her fingers through as she concentrated so she permanently looked as if she'd just got out of bed.

"So what's your worst habit?" she asked Dave in the canteen after he followed her blindly for coffee. "I grind my teeth at night," she said. "Terrible. I'll be a gummy old lady." She opened her mouth to show perfect American white teeth. It was only later, lying listening beside Eleanor as she slept, that he remembered she'd not given him the opportunity to reply. What would he have said anyway? None of the bad habits his ex-girlfriends criticised him for seemed appropriate for a first date, if that was what he and Eleanor had just had – he never committed to a plain yes or no, he called everybody he loved by pet dog names, his hands started sweating after you'd been holding them a while. He was surprised to realise how many bad habits he had. He could have gone on and on. It was like counting sheep. When he woke up with the shock of finding Eleanor already astride him, he was so grateful he vowed that this time he'd not spoil the relationship, that this one he wouldn't let go.

Big Boy and the Victim

Eleanor tells everyone about his weeping woman. Colin, who Dave has never liked, calls her one of de Beauvoir's bourgeois victims, lost in the pit of her own mediocrity. It's partly Eleanor's enthusiastic agreement that makes Dave argue. Normally he keeps his head down amongst Eleanor's friends.

"She wasn't ordinary," he argues. "She was ..." He pauses, temporarily lost for words.

"Suffocating? Needing to be rescued? And by such a big boy." Eleanor puts in just enough insinuation to make him blush.

"Bitch," he whispers. "She was just being human. Feminine even, but you wouldn't know about that, would you?"

Eleanor laughs, stuffing her fist in her mouth. He knows it's partly the shock of him fighting back than because she finds anything he's said funny. The worm turning.

He leaves the bar and walks home, careful to catch no woman's eye as he crosses the road.

The bulk of tissues can get in the way

The counsellor at couples therapy seems distracted. She keeps getting up, rearranging the curtains, pouring herself another glass of water, readjusting the small stool she's placed for her bad leg to rest on.

Dave looks at Eleanor, trying to catch her eye to share the joke, but she isn't having it. She's made it clear that the only way she's prepared to take him back is if he makes a serious effort to resolve his issues.

"You walked out on me," she has explained patiently, as if he hadn't been there, "in front of my friends. You called me bitch."

"But ..."

"Not this poor-little-me act again. Plee-eze. The question here is responsibility, Dave. You have to learn to stand up for yourself. Understand that wanting to rescue women is just another way of avoiding a full equal relationship."

He tries to make sense but can't, so listens instead to Eleanor explain his family background to the counsellor. He feels curiously detached from the situation until she starts to talk about his mother. He wants to interrupt and point out how funny his mother could be, how she used to make him and his father rock with laughter, how they conspired to give each other treats, but he's scared his mouth won't behave properly. It keeps forming the word Bitch and he mustn't let that out. Not now.

"They used his mother as a doll," Eleanor says, "as if she were some kind of prize for them being proper men. How could she get any grip on reality given that attitude?"

Dave remembers one time he and his mother coloured together. He was way past the age for colouring but he'd just been dumped by his first serious girlfriend and his mother hadn't tried to comfort him in the usual ways. Just gone to the drawer, brought out a tub of brightly coloured crayons and a book of pattern outlines and they'd spent the evening poring over their drawings, swapping colours, a bubble of shared concentration. The next morning, Dave had felt a shifting lightness, a gratitude towards his mother that had caused him to ache with love when he'd gone back to the drawer later that day.

It was easy to see from the number of completed pictures there that colouring was not something new for his mother, but he knew she wouldn't want him to ask her about it.

"Here." His reverie is broken by the counsellor pushing over a box of tissues. "Take as many as you want," she says. "I buy them in bulk."

Dave smiles at her and she smiles back, pushing her hair back behind her ears, so he can see better the unshed tears glisten in her eyes. Only Eleanor looks on frozen, her words suspended mid-sentence.

"It's been a hell of a morning," the counsellor tells him, ignoring Eleanor. "So you think you're the only one with problems."

Making Midnight Lists

Five things he's grateful to Eleanor for:

1. He visited his mother's grave for the first time after the visit to the counsellor.
2. He's taken up colouring again. And jigsaw puzzles.
3. If it wasn't for her, he wouldn't have finished his dissertation, wouldn't have got the new job in London.
4. She's given him her address in the States. She says they'll always have a connection. When he sorts himself out, she'll welcome a visit. She'd hate to know it, but she's given him an escape route.
5. The sex. Oh, the sex.

Five things he doesn't miss about Eleanor:

1. Quorn burgers without tomato ketchup.
2. Touching her skin in the middle of the night and having his fingers find those little dry bumpy patches on the downy skin just above her buttocks.
3. Having to buy the guide book for everywhere they visited.
4. Her friends, especially Colin.
5. Always being in the wrong.

Who are we to matter if our weight is immaterial?

Dave takes on a personal fitness trainer called Carl. He starts to go to the gym regularly for the first time in his life, and meets up with other gym users in the coffee bar after sessions. They discuss their personal trainers. Dave notices how these trainers are doubly personal in the sense they are often described with just the word 'mine' by their clients.

"Mine dropped beads of sweat on my chest today when I was doing sit ups," Dave says and everyone groans.

Dave hadn't minded. He'd wanted the sweat to be absorbed through his own pores, he wanted to feed off another man's jouissance. Carl is more alive than anyone Dave has met before. Even Eleanor who perspired only fleetingly and never drippingly.

Better than Arriving

He used to listen out for Santa's bells every Christmas Eve long after he stopped believing, long after even his mother stopped thinking he believed.

Now he stands on street corners. He can't admit this even to himself but what he's hoping for is for a strange woman to rest her hand on his arm.

Sometimes he waits there for hours, letting the tears stream down his cheeks.

Jesus and the Aubergines

My husband spent August wondering whether he wanted to leave me or not. I didn't seem to be involved in the decision, so I filled the time by going on a diet of raw vegetables. I followed the instructions exactly from a book I bought purely on the strength of the photograph on the front cover. It was of a model with long blonde hair, bright eyes and the sort of smile you thought could only belong to rich American children. I knew that wasn't true, because my husband had fallen in love with a girl with perfect white teeth and she came from Nottingham.

I loved that book. At a time when everything was falling down around me, it gave me rules to hold on to. I even had a task to do each day, with a little box to tick when I had finished. I don't think I've ever been so satisfied as when I was ticking those boxes. The book was just one of many things I lost when my husband finally left, but I can still remember one instruction.

"Place yourself directly in front of a market trader's stall and put your arms out in front of you at shoulder level. Then walk slowly towards the produce until your hands are an inch away from touching. Stand still for several minutes and you will be able to feel the vibrations of goodness moving directly from the vegetables to your own body."

I think it does you good to realise there are people so innocent that they think you can still do something like that in public and get away with it.

*

About six months later, I was at the supermarket. I prefer to go late in the evening so I can miss all those young mothers doing family shops. They look at my simple purchases with so much pity. I had just reached the vegetables when I was struck by a vision of a Jesus figure, arms raised, blessing the aubergines.

A gurgle rose up from me and I was away. I tried everything but I could not stop laughing. It was loud too, not the sort of watery chuckle you can get away with. My body was rocking so hard I had to hold on tight to the trolley with both hands and there were tears rolling down my cheeks. All I could think about were those bloody aubergines.

I could see him coming towards me from the other side of the carrots. He looked almost frightened in his blue suit and little white badge. 'Colin. Assistant Manager. Here to Help.' I was trying to concentrate on these small details in my effort to stop laughing.

"Is everything all right?" he said and I noticed he was trying to smile in a relaxed, confident way but because he was so nervous, his mouth kept twitching. I felt sorry for him. After all, he was probably only about twenty; just a couple of years older than my Calum. My pity must have done the trick because I could feel the laughter simmer down inside.

I nodded.

He looked relieved. "OK," he said, looking around at the crowd which had gathered. "Everything's under control." And everything would have been fine, if he hadn't then lifted up his arms in a gesture that was supposed to be a gentle reminder for people to disperse but was positioned directly above the aubergines. I started to laugh again, even harder this time although my stomach was aching and I had got a stitch. I put both hands on my waist to support myself. If only he could have seen what he looked like.

Colin held on to my elbow and tried to steer me away from the vegetables but I couldn't move. I felt so drained that even to me, my laughter sounded as if I was reading it out of a comic book: "Ho, ho, ho. Ha, ha, ha." I was aware of Colin looking around desperately for someone to help him.

"Shall I get you a nice cup of tea?" he asked, in the sort of voice you hope might soothe a child in mid-tantrum.

I nodded. It might have been a cliché but, to tell the truth, a nice cup of tea was precisely what I could do with at that moment.

We walked together to the supermarket cafe; his arm still on my elbow as if he was scared I was going to run away. I could feel his hand was wet and clammy and for the first time, I felt ashamed at putting him through this. At least I had stopped laughing. I was exhausted, collapsing into the seat Colin held out for me and gulping at my tea.

"Do you have anyone we could call?" He was still looking scared and I didn't blame him. I wasn't exactly the picture of reasonableness. I thought about my children and then rejected each in turn. Calum would be out with his university friends and Debbie was staying over at her friend Christine's. She spent all her time there nowadays. I had called it the hippy, happy house once because of all the windchimes and burning candles Christine's mother has around, but Debbie didn't laugh.

"What about your husband?" Colin was still prodding, anxious to get rid of me onto someone else.

"My ex-husband is probably out on the town somewhere," I said, "pretending to be twenty years younger than he is." The bitterness was so habitual I was surprised to see Colin flinch. "Don't mind me," I tried to reassure him. "I'm just an old mad woman who goes wild in the veggie department."

"What was so funny?" He was smiling at me now. It was as if it took me mocking my own sanity to reassure him I was all right.

I thought about telling him about the book and about Jesus and the vibrating vegetables, but I knew he wouldn't understand. "Just a joke someone told me about aubergines," I said. I was trying to look as if this explained everything, but I needn't have bothered. I could tell he was thinking about something else.

"My mum and dad are divorced," he said. "They split up when I was seventeen."

"Divorce is hard for everybody," I said quickly. I was still feeling too sorry for myself to be interested in anyone else's pain.

"Dad ran off with someone younger." He was stirring his coffee round and round, gazing into the circles he'd made on the black liquid surface. "Someone my age."

"All men are fools." I said it automatically. I wanted to leave now, get back home. I'd do my shopping at another supermarket the next day.

"Not just someone my age. Someone I knew. Someone I'd been to school with."

"Was she your girlfriend?" He'd caught my attention now. I think I'd have killed my husband if he'd run off with one of Calum's girlfriends.

He shook his head. "She wouldn't even look at me," he said. "Latched on to my dad though. She knew which side her bread was buttered on."

I decided to be brisk. I didn't want Colin collapsing on me. "Well, you've done very nicely for yourself now," I said. "I bet your mum is proud of you."

He raised his head at that, giving me a long steady look which was meant to let me know he had taken in my expensive clothes and respectable haircut. "Would you be happy if your children were working in a shop like this?" he said.

I thought about it. Once I might have said I didn't care what my children did so long as they were happy, but now I had failed as a wife, it was the fact that my children had glittering lives ahead of them that kept me going. Especially my daughter. Especially Debbie.

"I'm sorry," I said. "I didn't think."

He shrugged his shoulders. "Mum keeps on at me," he said. "Get a better job, she says. Finish your studies and show your father what you're made of, but you get used to the money, I suppose."

I got up, leaving half my tea in the cup. It was cold anyway. "I wish you well, Colin. Thank you for your time."

He stayed in his seat, so I was left standing above him. "It's the structure I like," he said. "I know what to expect here. There are rules for everything - from the way we put the fruit on display to the number of coffee breaks we can take. I don't know where I'd be without that."

I put my hand on his shoulder. Such vulnerability should not be allowed to show. He twisted in his chair to look up at me. "And then you came along..." He sounded almost aggrieved. "I'd never had something happen like that before; something I couldn't deal with. It shook me."

"You were fine. Very, very..." I struggled for the word that would make him feel better. "You were very managerial."

He smiled at that. He was too clever not to know what I was doing, but young enough to want to take my compliment at face value. "And you're really feeling better?"

I nodded. "I'm going to go home now to sort myself out. I must look a mess."

He didn't contradict me but just held out his hand awkwardly. "It's been very nice meeting you," he said.

"And you, Colin," I replied and then hesitated. "Give my best wishes to your mother, Colin. I know what it must be like for you both."

*

I didn't want to face an empty house, so I just drove around in circles. It was the time of night when people put on their lights but don't draw their curtains so I was able to catch glimpses into people's lives - a woman plumping up a cushion and once, heartstoppingly, a man staring directly out at me from the window.

When it started to rain, I went to pick up Debbie, making no excuses for the change of plan. She came quickly enough, but not before throwing Christine one of those looks which are heavy with hidden meanings. For the first time, I realised that she must discuss me with her friends. I had been so proud of the way I had kept up my front in public. In fact, that feeling of privacy was one of the things that I had left but I couldn't feel cross with her. I was probably the last person she could have talked to.

"Where's the shopping?" Debbie asked, turning round in the car to look.

"I didn't have time," I lied. "Let's go tomorrow, shall we? Choose some special treats. Everything we haven't allowed ourselves for ages. We'll make pigs of ourselves."

She laughed. A proper girl's laugh of the kind I hadn't heard from her in months. "Do you remember those raw salads you used to eat, Mum?" she said. "They were the end, weren't they?"

I concentrated on the road ahead, watching the windscreen wipers curve across the window. Following their rhythm, I began to chant: "Fudge bars, chocolate ice cream, sausages, marshmallows, pot noodles ..."

Debbie joined in. "Tinned soup, baked beans, marzipan..."

I looked over at my daughter. I had forgotten how quick she was to pick up my jokes. Even now, she was smiling at me as if I really could make it all better. I thought of Colin, pacing the aisles, carefully pricing and counting his cans.

"Jelly Beans!" I shouted. "We shall have lots and lots of Jelly Beans for breakfast."

"Are we allowed?" Debbie looked at me, hopefully. She was too young for all this, I thought.

"What would you most like to eat for breakfast? Don't even think if you'll be allowed it or not," I asked.

She shouted it out. "Christmas pudding!"

I pulled the car over to the side and swung it round in a U-turn.

"Where are we going now?" she said.

"To the supermarket, of course," I replied. "If you want Christmas pudding for breakfast, then we'd better buy some for when you wake up."

She smiled at me. "Do you know what Christine's mother says?"

"No. What does Christine's mother say?"

"She says..." Debbie was looking at me, suddenly unsure how I would take this. With a sinking feeling, I knew that Christine's mother had been talking about me as well.

"Go on," I said with a cheerfulness I did not feel.

"She says that life is too short not to forgive." I could hear Debbie expel the breath she had been holding in.

I laughed. Christine's mother was an earth mother, a frustrated sixties child. I could just imagine her saying that.

"She's right," I said, and Debbie looked so relieved that I couldn't help but wonder what the last year had been like for her. I put my hand on hers, and she unclenched her fist to hold mine as easily as if she had been a small child again.

"What does Christine's mother have for breakfast?" I asked and Debbie snorted, giggling.

"Raw carrots and grated apples," she said and I had to turn my head away to smile.

"The end," I said. "The absolute end."

A Lovely Evening

There is an air of celebration across the small suburban town. Three parties are being held this night.

Outside a small well-lit bungalow, fourteen year old Susan Bentall is being sick into a pink rosebush while Paul McCrae watches. He swears at Susan as he fails once again to inhale the smoke from his cigarette without coughing.

In a cul-de-sac round the corner, ten sixty-year-olds sit down at a table highly polished in the way only Mr Phillips knows how to get just right. Mrs Phillips, although adequate in the kitchen, never manages to get things exactly as her husband prefers. Wine flows into crystal glasses brought in Ireland that summer to replace the set given as a wedding present, long since chipped and discarded. When Mrs Phillips brings the crème brulee to the table she pauses for her husband to make his joke - got the ice pick, dear - and only then does she expel the breath she's been holding all evening.

Meanwhile over the other side of town, men and women half their age circle each other in the desperate knowledge that time is running out. Most are divorced; "living proof that optimism never dies," someone says. Kate Armstrong and Geoff Carter connect over the dried out party food and the fact that they had both enjoyed the pathos of *Au Revoir Les Enfants*. Geoff forgives Kate her mispronunciation of the title as he watches her fingers echo the shape and figure of that small, vulnerable child.

At the same moment as Paul swears at the clasp of Susan's bra and Mrs Phillips catches her husband's eye and wonders again how much longer she will be forced to live, Geoff offers Kate a lift home. And maybe a quick cup of coffee. It is so noisy at the party and they have so much in common.

In the car, Kate tells Geoff her dreams.

She wants to because he is a writer too and will understand them. She tells him that she has fallen in love with the way he says them back to her. Kate watches Geoff's mouth move, his lips stretch over those perfect straight teeth and in the middle of a phrase, a word even, she says kiss me. And after they do, the pity Kate feels for everyone else that night, for everyone alone that night, for the Kate that is normally alone, is so strong she leans back in her seat and just watches Geoff drive.

And then, dry and safe inside his flat, they carry on talking about nothing, about everything, as she prowls the room, lifting the glass of red wine to her face and just smelling the rim, not ready to take anything just yet.

I want to drape fairy lights around your furniture, Kate tells Geoff, put white flowers in earthenware pots in every corner of your room, read you sonnets and explain their rhythm to you, tap out the sequence on your bare skin, tell you why that word and not that one. She stands in the doorway of Geoff's kitchen and breathes in the good smells. A man who can cook. I want, she says.

Geoff wonders if he can force himself to make the effort. He thinks of Siobhan who told him dreams were boring. Who had never read a poem. Who ate her meals without comment. And all he really wants to do was to crawl into bed. On his own. He chops the peppers hard, squashes the tomatoes between his fingers into the saucepan. There's no reason at least why he shouldn't have a good meal. What are you doing, he asks as he hears shuffling footsteps in the next room, books rustling and - surely not - drawers opening.

I want to drape fairy lights around you, he hears her say, as she comes towards him, to where he is standing, fondling the handle of his kitchen knife.

Coffee everyone, asks Mrs Phillips, no don't worry I'll make it on my own quite happy just carry on enjoy yourself we're lucky to have you yes really I'm fine. And as Mr Phillips nods at her to hurry up she thinks I want to kill you. Such a lovely evening, she says.

Paul lays Susan down on the edge of some wasteland and tells her that he'll love her for ever and she asks really, really and he says yes really hold me there there touch me there. Love, says Susan, my love.

Kate tells Geoff that when he looks at her so gently, he stills her. Turns off every clock she has ticking inside. You are my Sunday rest, she tells him. You are not a stranger, you are not a lover. You are my father.

Siobhan, screams Geoff, not knowing from which corner of his body the name comes from but he is too far away. No one hears. No one ever does.

Mrs Phillips ignores her husband tapping his spoon against his cup for too long and is rewarded by the sight of his arm worming its way around Trixie Ward's shoulder. She watches Mr Phillips' hand caressing the fold of fat beneath Trixie's armpit and the shelf of her tight, too young silk dress and knows that this is a route it has followed before, a map it knows by heart. More coffee, Mrs Phillips says brightly, no no one move please just a little accident silly me no use crying over spilt milk.

Paul wonders if it would be better if Susan was more responsive. It's uncomfortable the way he has to bend and shape her body himself, and once by mistake he lets his face get too near her mouth where her open lips are crying out for more than he can ever give. Bitch, he whispers into her shoulder. Oh bitch, don't make me come too quickly. You're just like all the others, bitch.

Your father, Geoff asks and Kate laughs. You are the other half of my soul I've been searching for, she says. We should mark this moment, spill not seed but blood. Do something, make something that no one will expect of us. Spittle, sperm, blood. These are the fluids we should mix tonight. I want to get to know every bit of your body, inside and out.

Siobhan was a thief. When she left Geoff, she stole every moment like this from his future. Truly, madly, deeply. Red roses and blue violets. The heart wants what the heart wants. And what Geoff's heart wants just then is to be left alone to grieve. To find its own way back into Geoff's body. To slip into the warm shell that is so empty without it. That is proving so feeble at repelling invaders.

We've been waiting so long for each other, Kate tells Geoff. Welcome home.

There's a big gap at the table where Mr Phillips and Trixie Ward have been sitting. Mrs Phillips's stomach jumps across the blankness as she lets her gaze swing round and round the table. Her life is sitting in this room, discussing property values, golf handicaps and surely too young difficult to believe but yes grandchildren love them dearly you'll never guess what little Emily is doing now.

Susan Bentall dreams that Paul is carrying her down the altar under a canopy of twinkling stars. I'll never leave you, he says and as she curls her body up into itself, the empty legs of her jeans shadow her pose on the rough ground beside her, the damp seeping through the thin denim so when she will wake up in the morning and have to put them on they will rub even harder into the sore skin between her legs as she runs, stumbling, home.

At midnight Geoff lies back on his bed and shuts his eyes. Trust me, he hears, and for a moment he thinks it is Siobhan, his girl, come back to him so he offers no defence. Take me, he tells her, and the words sing through every town, in every land, rustling through trees, called by the birds and written in the clouds. Just take me away. Anywhere but here.

And back in that quiet cul-de-sac in the middle of the small sub-urban town, Mr and Mrs Phillips stand on their doorstep and wish their guests a pleasant journey home. It's been such a lovely evening. A lovely evening, Mrs Phillips echoes as she follows her husband back into the house and waits patiently while he double locks the door.

The Fabulous Button Sisters

It was the afternoon before Rory's party and I was lying on my bed, when the phone started ringing downstairs. I could hear Mum shout "Karen, it's for you," without even bothering to pick it up. As I clattered down the stairs, she and Dad were laughing in the kitchen.

"I'm thinking buttons." It was my friend, Michelle. "Chocolate ones."

This was one of the good things about her. The way she always plunged right into the middle of a sentence, of a story, of a friendship even. She knew I'd know who she was, just as Mum knew I'd know. It was better than the boring way I took my time, needing things spelt out. Not like Michelle. She just leapt.

"Sorry?" I asked.

Michelle wasn't supposed to be my best friend even. She was the new girl at school the term my proper best friend Connie was off with glandular fever, but from the minute she walked in to the classroom, I was in love. It wasn't just her lip gloss, or the way no bossy parent told her what to do, or even that she was living with an aunt who read American magazines, offered Michelle cigarettes, had boyfriends and, Michelle said, thirty two pairs of different coloured high heeled shoes. No, it was the way she took over any space going. Made it her own.

And by the time Connie came back, Michelle had made me hers. There was no other expression for it. "We can still be friends at weekends and after school," I whispered to Connie but

I couldn't hide my relief when Michelle just booked us both in for every club going until she thought it was safe to let me have some free time. Any decision I might have to make between Connie and Michelle was taken out of my hands.

It didn't take long to realise that owning things was more important to Michelle than me. "Own the stage, Karen," she hissed once much later when I had to go up to the front of the maths class to finish the problem on the board. "Own the track," she shouted out to me in athletics when I was trailing behind in the 800 metres. "Own the pavement," she used to despair when I found myself knocked into the gutter for the umpteenth time as we walked into town together.

"We'll dress up as buttons. I'll be white and you can be ordinary," Michelle said now.

"But what if I want to be white?" I didn't particularly. Well, I didn't particularly want to be any colour of chocolate button, but that wasn't to say there couldn't be a what if.

"Don't be silly," Michelle said. "Besides your mum always wears brown, doesn't she? So you'll have lots of clothes to choose from."

This was true. Despite my hints, I'd never actually met Michelle's aunt but I'd take a bet she wouldn't wear muddy hues. I hummed a bit to give myself time to think.

"Look." Michelle could be very patient when she wanted. "Look," she repeated, "it's me that's taking the risk here. After all, brown can fade into the background, but white? White makes a statement. No one is going to notice you."

There was something wrong with this I couldn't quite put my finger on.

"We'll be the Fabulous Button Sisters," Michelle was saying.

She was always trying to get us to be the Fabulous Something Sisters. Apparently to make an impression, it was important to have a Unique Image. This was the type of thing Michelle knew about because much as she loved her aunt, she was only staying with her until her mum broke into Hollywood. Michelle's mum was even more glamorous, had even more pairs of shoes, but apparently however fabulous you were, it was hard to do the breaking in bit with a teenage daughter hanging around. Although Michelle's mum had been young – almost a baby herself – when she'd had her, it still made her look too old. As soon as she'd made it big though, she was going to bring Michelle over and make her a star too. That was why Michelle had to be prepared. Me too, because Michelle said I had to go with her now. After all, we were a double act now, weren't we? The Fabulous Something Sisters.

"Are you still there?" Michelle was shouting down the phone.

"The Fabulous Button Sisters," I repeated, as much for something to say as anything else. "Who are they then?"

"Us," Michelle said simply. "It'll be like a party game. People will have to guess who we are. We'll be a sensation. And, if I can be honest here, you need some practise on your charisma."

There was no point arguing after that. I went to raid Mum's wardrobe.

"They seem a bit dull," Mum said doubtfully, watching me try on a dirt-coloured skirt and beige top. "Call me old-fashioned but we used to want to dress up for parties when I was your age."

I didn't tell her about Michelle's theme because I guessed what she'd say. I hadn't told Mum about going to America yet. The trouble was that to Mum, variety meant different kinds of vegetables rather than anything to do with the theatre. She wasn't like Michelle's mum. She wouldn't understand. "We've got a kind of anti-fabulous thing going," I lied. The words rolled off my tongue like melted chocolate.

Mum nodded as if she understood, but afterwards, she and Dad were laughing so hard they didn't hear me come downstairs and stand outside the door. "Anti-fabulous," Dad was

was wheezing. "And to think she wanted your clothes for that, pet."

At least that stopped Mum guffawing quite so much. "I wish she'd wouldn't see so much of Michelle," she said. "I know you've got to be kind, but our Karen seems so wan these days. It's as if she's fading away, or something."

I burst through the door then before she could get off on one of her fits about my eating habits. Michelle said it was important we kept up to date with diets. Two weeks ago, she decided that we were only going to eat one colour of food at every meal. She'd got the idea from one of her aunt's magazines. Apparently everybody was doing it. Mum and Dad stopped talking when I came into the kitchen watching as I carefully cut the brown crust off the bread and spread the white inside with butter and cream cheese.

"How about a nice bit of ham with that?" Mum asked.

I shook my head. When I'd first tried to explain about the mono-colour diet, Mum had looked at me with the kind of expression which meant she was storing it up to giggle about with Dad later.

"Or some pickle." Dad was already moving towards the store cupboard. "There's some fabulous..." He couldn't continue. He stuck his head inside the cupboard but I could see his shoulders moving up and down. Mum busied herself tidying up the papers on the table. Parents could be so childish sometimes.

I took my white sandwich upstairs to my bedroom, slamming the door, only half-accidentally, on the way out.

Michelle thought my parents had a problem with repressed anger. This was why they laughed so much and spent so much time together in such an unhealthy way. She learnt all about anger when her father had left home. Apparently he hadn't wanted Michelle's mother to become a big star and grow away from him.

"But he lost her anyway by leaving," I said, trying to figure this one out.

"Yes," Michelle explained patiently, "but by being the one to go first, he took ownership of the situation."

I'd tried to look as if I'd understood, but I couldn't get rid of the feeling that her dad had still lost out somehow.

"And then your mum left as well?" I asked.

Michelle nodded.

"So what was she owning?"

Michelle didn't reply, just started flicking through one of the magazines we were always surrounded by. Together we usually dissected the celebrities, criticising their legs, or dresses, or hair in turn, and Michelle told me how much better looking her Mum was than any of them. She was teaching me good taste, although the ones she always liked best were the sisters – Paris and Lisa, Mary Kate and Ashley. When we found pictures of them together, we had to stand in front of the mirror to copy the poses. What I found hard was to get exactly the right distance to stand behind Michelle. I kept catching my worried expression looming over her shoulder in the glass.

Up in my bedroom, I stuffed the last piece of white bread in my mouth, and stood up to pull on my brown chocolate outfit. I stood in front of the mirror and stared. Mum was right. I looked dull. I tried to imagine Michelle standing in front of me in her white outfit and it felt better so this time I gave us both a big bright smile.

Downstairs I could hear the phone. "Karen, it's for you," Mum shouted as it carried on ringing. I bounded down the stairs two by two to get it.

"Ten minutes," Michelle said. "Meet you on the corner."

But when I walked down the street towards her, a chocolate button searching for the rest of the packet, something had gone wrong. Michelle was wearing a green sequined top and pleated denim miniskirt. Her hair was pinned up and she had sparkling earrings on. The way she glittered under the street lamp made me guess she'd practised exactly where to stand to make the light fall on her.

"Guess what," she shouted, although I was only about six inches away from her. She was waving an envelope in my face so I took it. "Mum wants me to join her at long last. She's sending my tickets this week. She thinks I'm ready."

"So what have you come as?" I asked. "A green mouldy button?"

It wasn't that I was ignoring what she'd just said. I was confused. What about me? We were going to America together, weren't we? Because wasn't that what it was all about? Our double act. The fabulous sisters.

"I'm just an ordinary girl going to her last ordinary party before she hits the big time. I'm moving on," Michelle said. But then she looked at me and put her hand up to her forehead. "Oh my god, I'd forgotten. We were going to get dressed up, weren't we?" Her smile made me think she'd already moved far away from me and was remembering something quaint and old-fashioned. "Still, you look nice," she lied.

I spent the party huddled in the kitchen, invisible in Mum's brown clothes, while Michelle dazzled, and shone, and lit up the room, forcing the rest of us backstage. It was clear there was room for only one under her spotlight.

She'd asked me to keep her mother's letter for safekeeping and I'd thrust it into one of my pockets. Now I pounced on people bringing glasses through for washing up so I wouldn't have to read it again. Connie slouched in at one point, her shoulders hunched in her grey sweatshirt. I wanted to tell her to stand up straight, to walk tall just as Michelle had taught me. Own the kitchen, I could imagine Michelle saying. My shoulders went back automatically, my smile dazzling but then I remembered and let them fall.

"Is something wrong?" Connie asked worriedly, and I shook my head. She lingered for a moment, and then muttered something about how lovely Michelle looked. I nodded.

"Michelle and I," I stuttered, "we're not really like sisters any more, Connie. In fact, I'm not sure we ever really were."

This was when I could have told her everything, put the whole thing in her lap to sort out for me, but Connie smiled then, her funny gentle smile that wouldn't light up any stage.

"You move on, don't you?" I said instead briskly, and I tried not to think about how people like me and Connie rarely moved on. Not unless we were pushed. This made me feel sad too. I didn't even watch as she drifted back to the party.

For the first month after she'd gone, Michelle kept sending me postcards with pictures of Hollywood stars on the front. She talked about how well she and her mother were getting on, almost like sisters, she said, and how fabulous it all was.

"You'd love Mum," Michelle wrote. "We could be a trio." When Michelle signed her name she drew a little smiley face, but the smile was all wobbly so it looked as if it was mocking both of us. I showed the postcards off to Connie and the gang at first though and kept on buying the magazines myself so I could practise the poses and follow the diets to be ready when Michelle finally called for me to join her, but it was hard to keep the same magic going.

As I gradually gave up, Mum and Dad stopped laughing at me quite so much and although I kept telling myself how lovely it was to be back to being ordinary, I couldn't get rid of the feeling that a part of me was missing.

It wasn't just that I could wear what I wanted, eat what I wanted; no, it was the way everyone kept giving me time to come up with my own ideas. Ideas like remembering how the letter from Michelle's mother that I'd seen at the party was postmarked not from Hollywood but Birmingham, England, and that was the same as the postcards I got from Michelle.

When I didn't reply, the postcards stopped coming. I tried to take comfort at how at least this way Michelle would have been proud of me. But all I could think about was how I would have liked to tell her how I had finally learnt to take ownership of something. Even if it was just the situation.

Lonesome Tonight

It's the collective gasp that gets me.

That particular noise you get when a crowd gathers to watch fireworks or some particularly dangerous acrobatic display and everyone goes "oooo" together. They just open their mouths slightly so there's a tiny hole in the middle where their lips don't quite meet and they expel a minute puff of air. Oooo. It's that precise. Not oh or ow but oooo. And you're all doing it together. You're part of a group. It's a great feeling.

Sylvia claims my fear of solitude is really a fear of death. Of not facing up to facts. "It's going to happen to us all some time," she says. "And when you go, you go alone. Better get used it now while you can practise."

And that afternoon proves Sylvia right. There we all are, a crowd of about ten to fifteen people breathing in unison as we watch a man jump out of a window. We're part of the same machine. One minute, our main concern is the successful negotiation of the journey from sandwich bar back to office without catching anyone else's eye; the next we're holding hands, clutching at strangers' arms. Oooo.

But him, he's on his own. He means business. If it had been me, I think I would have just tip-toed off the ledge, even at the last minute hoping to hit something solid with the next step but not him. He jumps right out there, looking straight ahead.

He even holds his arms high above his head to resist any temptation to break his fall.

"There was nothing we could do," I say to the woman standing next to me. A tear is trickling down her cheek but she makes no effort to wipe it away. Her arms are clutching a used supermarket bag to her chest so tightly, I worry she must be hurting herself. She's still looking up at where the man had been. If she hadn't shaken her head slightly, I might have thought she was frozen. I look up too, wondering what she can see that I can't; what she can feel that I seem to be missing out on. I blink tightly, trying to will a tear to fall from my eyes too, hoping it will make me feel more involved. When nothing comes, I snap the red elastic bands I wear on my arm hard against my skin. Eventually the way they sting makes my eyes water. I catch my neighbour's eye and she smiles sympathetically. At last, we are sharing something.

We stand like that for a moment, and I think it's not because we can do anything but because we don't want to let go of that group feeling. I am certainly not going to be the first to move away. Being on your own is dangerous. We'd just seen proof of that.

"Someone's going to be lonesome tonight," a bicycle messenger then half-sings, half-whispers from underneath his peaked helmet. It sounds like a curse and so, by the time the policeman moves forward to break us up, we're ready to leave anyway.

Sylvia is my mother. She was a regular juice-and-biscuits mummy once, but when I got to twenty and still hadn't left home, she decided that things had to change. We're flatmates now. We share the bills, chores and emotional caring equally. Lines have been drawn over which I am not to cross. I get my own back by refusing to call her Sylvia. I like the way she blanches every time I use the word 'Mum'.

"I've had enough maternal martyrdom for the rest of my life," she tells me, fluttering a carefully drawn grid of rules in front of my eyes before she pins it up in the kitchen.

Rule no 1. We will not suck the life-blood from the other.

I look up at her and then read on. And on.

Rule no 9. Privacy will be strictly guarded, particularly as far as overnight visitors are concerned.

I am puzzled by Rule no 9. Nowadays, the only people who visit my mother are men she doesn't introduce me to. None of them ever stay overnight because their wives like them to read bed-time stories to their children.

"When you say overnight, do you really mean during sex?" I ask.

"Christina!" She looks around quickly before she re-members it is just me and her in the room. She may not be called Mum any more but she is still proof that changing your name overnight can't change your habits. I can see she has to make a conscious effort to switch back to Sylvia mode.

"Anyway, you might want to bring someone home with you one night," she says.

I can't bear the look of hope in her eyes. "I might still want a mother," I tell her quickly. "I may not have had enough maternal martyring."

"Think of other people sometimes," she says. "You can't hang on to me for the rest of your life."

I want to ask why not, but I'm scared of what she might say. Instead, I tell her about the man jumping from the window. I know she'll like the story and indeed, her mouth falls open in a satisfying way. I embroider wildly, claiming that he looked straight into my eyes before he plunged, that the electricity had sparkled between us and I known immediately that if he'd lived, we'd have been soulmates. "Help me," I tell her he'd cried as he tumbled down, his arms outstretched just for me. The words had flown straight into my heart like splinters of ice. I'd wanted to run out from the crowd and hold out my skirts to catch him, I say.

Sylvia has a far-off look in her eyes. "I wonder how they told the people who loved him," she says.

"He had one of those identity card things on a chain around his neck," I remember. "They'll be able to identify him by that and contact his home. I suppose they'd visit personally for a death."

She looks at me as if she hates me. "No, I mean his real love," she says. "There might be someone waiting for him right now, wondering why the phone doesn't ring, why there's no knock at the door. She must be in so much pain right now. No one would think to tell her."

I don't care about that. I am still so caught up in the memory of the shared suffering that my first feeling is fury that once again, my mother is ignoring my pain.

"Mum," I say slowly, trying to think of a way I could really hurt her. "Who would they tell first if it was Dad who jumped out of the window?"

If I stand a little to one side, I can watch my mother from the bedroom window without being spotted. She is in the garden, praying to the Mother Goddess. I used to do this with her once upon a time but nothing I wished for ever came true so I gave up. I couldn't see that anything good had happened for my mother either but that didn't seem to worry her.

She's bending her knees slightly, both feet planted solidly on the ground. Her right hand reaches down to the earth and then slowly, painstakingly she moves it up the side of her body before throwing it open, right up to the skies. I can't hear but I can see her mouth move round the magic word. "Sha!"

81

Sylvia likes to tell people she's a witch. It's part of the campaign she's been conducting to make herself more interesting since my father left us.

"I don't know why you bother," I tell her when I come down one morning to find the breakfast table covered with magic-making white candles, crystals and scraps of red ribbon. "Nothing's going to bring Dad back now."

"When the time is right," she says, "mountains may move."

I laugh. I can't help it. "Janice is a bit like a mountain," I admit and even Sylvia smiles then. She likes me to be rude about Janice, but she says she won't lower herself to common insult. I think it's because it's too easy. Even my father admits that Janice's main attraction is what he calls her 'ease'. He moved straight in with her after leaving us and when I lie in bed sometimes listening to my mother pace the floor downstairs, lighting cigarettes, constantly changing the music, I can understand him completely. The differences between living with Janice and my mother must be like entering a blood warm plunge pool after the rigours of the sauna and icy dip. Every time I think of Janice, I imagine her lying on the sofa eating soft-centred chocolates. Making love to her must be like entering a perfectly baked Victoria sandwich cake. She even smells of vanilla. Yes, I could see the attraction. There are times when even I find it hard to resist the erotic urge to insert my hands into the folds of fat which make up Janice's body.

My mother hasn't found the spell which will make the telephone ring on cue. I catch her staring at it sometimes when we're supposed to be watching television and I can read her mind. She's got a picture of Dad there and she's trying to force him to ring her up. It hurts me to be in the same room as her then because even when it does go, it's never him. Or if it is, he can never speak for long enough to satisfy her.

I have to hand it to her though. She never gives up. I find a little list by the side of the phone. It reads:

Scf Bt Hrs / Mn Wm CD Trl HMV / Gl Mlk Bt.

She blushes when I show it to her.

"I'm going to tell Dad if this goes on," I say. "Magic's not fair."

"Have you never been in love?" she asks me.

"'*Better by far you should forget and smile, Than that you should remember and be sad*,'" I quote.

"You can't take over someone else's words and pretend it's you who's got a soul." She walks out of the room but I follow her because I could tell she wasn't finished. "We would never have called you Christina if we had known this was going to happen."

"'*Tell me of our future that you plann'd*,'" I say and she turns on me.

"Anyway, that's not a spell," she says, pointing at the scribbled note I still held in my hand. "It's to remind me of things to tell your father about."

I look at her and then again at the note. Like so much about my mother, it makes absolutely no sense at all.

She sighs theatrically and takes it back from me. "Look," she says, pointing the letters out just like she used to when I was learning to read. "This is about how that scaffolder put a bet on the grey at Ascot for me because he said I walked down the street like a race horse." I nod, wanting her to go on. "Then I wanted to tell him about how I saw a man and a woman load up a shopping trolley with CDs the last time I went to HMV. They weren't even looking at the names half the time, just shoving the CDs in straight from the shelves. There must have been hundreds there."

"Perhaps they'd won a competition?" I say.

"Exactly." My mother is getting into her stride now. "It's the sort of thing you see and want to share with other people.

The little snippets your father and I used to keep for each other."

"You could have told me about it," I point out. "I told you about the man jumping from the window."

My mother ignores this. "And this one is the milk bottle I saw on my way to work the other day. Someone had painted it gold. I knew Dad would like that one."

"Don't you think it's a little forced?" I ask. "Shouldn't conversation just come naturally?"

She looks at me pityingly. "When you get older, you'll realise that nothing comes naturally," she says. "If anything, you've got to work harder with the people you love so you can be the sort of person they want you to be."

"Janice isn't exactly working hard." I say, thinking of a strawberry cream chocolate trickling down that fat white throat. "She just is. She's like a proper mother."

My mother's face freezes. "There's a difference between just existing and real mothering," she says. "Janice hasn't the sensitivity to be a mother and you must stop idealising what it's like to be a daughter. What you need to do, Christina, is to grow up and find out who you really are before it's too late."

"'*The pulse of hope shall cease, Of joy and of regretting,*'" I say.

"Someone else's words." Sylvia shakes her head. "Find your own soul."

Now, looking at my mother in the garden I can't help wondering what she's wishing for. I am half-tempted to go out and join her in the garden and pray for a soul all of my own. Rolling backwards and forwards on the balls of my feet, I mirror her actions unconsciously, raising my own right hand to the ceiling and throwing my desires up into the air.

Above my head, my arm is covered in the rubber bands. I have devised a walk which takes me past all the post boxes in the area. The postmen round here must just throw the bands down on the ground when they take the letters out because over

84

the last week, I've collected enough to cover from my wrist to just below my elbow. I'm going to start on my ankles soon. Any part of me that's not protected my clothes. I use them as armour against my mother's magic. You see, I still hope she thinks of me.

When the phone rings, I find it difficult at first to bend my elbow to pick up the receiver and as I reach down, I notice the note lying on the small table in the hall.

Mn Jmp Wnd.

Someone else's words. My story. I feel such a surge of anger that I shout "Yes" down the phone without thinking.

It's Janice. Recently I've been encouraging her to ring me up to ask my advice about how she can make my father happy. "Do nothing. Just sit there and wait for him," I told her once. It was advice that seemed to have worked because he kept coming back to her and not to us.

I like Janice's voice. It has a soft, caressing undertone like the taste of caramel on the roof of your mouth. "Hello Christina," she purrs.

I close my eyes to listen better as the door slams behind me. Syliva comes bounding into the kitchen from the garden. We have no soft furnishings, not even carpets, so her every movement sends sharp slivers of sound through the house. The speed with which she reacts to the phone suddenly makes me realise I've known all along what she's been praying to the Mother Goddess for. How could I have ever hoped it was me?

"Hello Janice," I raise my voice slightly to make sure Sylvia could hear, but shift slightly round so my back is too her and she can't see the phone. "You want me to come round for a proper family supper? Of course I'd love to. No, Sylvia won't mind. She's always saying she has her own life to lead now."

The silence behind me is so heavy, I can tell Sylvia is listening. Listening so hard she has forgotten to breathe.

"Yes," I continue, my heart pounding. "I think of you as my family, too. You, me and Dad."

It's only then that I take my finger off the talk button so the dial sound fills my ears. My mother is right. Loving someone does mean that there are times you have to say the things they want you to say. Be the person they want you to be. I turn round just in time to see her dark figure hurrying back out to the garden.

Janice will think I am mad cutting her off like that, but this time, it is my own words that are important. If there's one thing my mother has taught me it is that there is some magic you have to weave yourself.

I go upstairs and stand at my bedroom window, watching my mother move back across the lawn. When I press both hands on it the frame pushes up easily and I climb onto the ledge and stand there, breathing in the night air. I lift my arms above my head, mirroring my mother's moon dance. I want to shut my eyes but I force myself to look ahead. I don't tiptoe but step right out, as if the space between my foot and the ground is a cushion I can sink right into.

I want to shout but there's no need. Sylvia is already looking at me. Really at me. When I land in the flowerbed, she holds out her hand and I take it, conscious how, for once, we're both gripping too tightly.

The Woman Downstairs

I have a woman stuck in my cellar. Well, not stuck. Locked there. By me. I pushed her down the stairs, switched off the light and turned the key.

She's been down there for three hours now, and I've spent the time sitting upstairs, wondering how I'm going to let her out. My husband will be home soon. He'll want a cup of tea. The kids need their things sorted out for tomorrow. And what if she starts banging? Someone's bound to notice and it will be hard to explain.

To be honest, I'm wondering myself why she's there. It's not as if she's just a strange woman either. She is Rebecca's mother so I can't claim self-protection. Can't say she tried to attack me. She comes to the house quite often and I've never locked her in the basement before.

The funny thing is it's less lonely with her down there. I don't normally have time to sit anywhere during the day. Now though, I'm not even reading a book. Just watching the shadows on the wall. They're dancing, stretching and contracting as the sun goes down. I don't think I've ever noticed them before.

It's a new sofa I'm sitting on. Nice and deep. Just right for pulling your legs up under you. I chose it myself. Peter and I used to make joint decisions about everything but recently he's left the domestic stuff to me. Says I'm better at it. And he's so busy. I can understand it, but can't help wishing sometimes... oh you know.

Still, it's a lovely sofa. Deep red with little patterns in the material that your fingers just long to run over. I sometimes watch television or listen to Peter tell me about his day and really I'm just stroking these little twists and bubbles of thread. Makes me think of when I was a kid and used to keep a scrap of my mother's apron in my blazer pocket at school. When things got tough, I'd just clutch at it, knowing there was another life somewhere else. That this wasn't all I'd got.

I'll need to let her out soon. If I can do that, I can do anything. I shall treat it as a joke. Pretend it was a childish prank and then I forgot all about her.

Mary's her name. The woman in my cellar.

*

I've just been down to see her. Took her some food. A nice cup of tea.

She was upset but I think I cheered her up. You do what you can. I started to sing her some of those old lullabies that used to soothe the kids. It's funny how many there are about Mary's. *Mary, Mary, quite contrary, how does your garden grow?* I told her we could have a few plants down there in the cellar. Make a garden of our own.

*

Even before Mary came to stay downstairs, I couldn't leave the house. I'd try but then I'd get to the front door and I couldn't go any further. It's like there's a wall there, stopping me. My heart starts to pound and it won't stop until I tell myself OK, you don't have to do this today. Tomorrow you can go out, but you don't have to do this today.

I come upstairs then. There's a box of photographs I like to look through. They're my window to the outside.

Here's one of a bride and a bridegroom standing at the top of a flight of stone steps leading to a garden. The woman is small, her dark curls escaping from behind her veil. Behind her, the new husband looks happy too, but more nervous. He looks raw. Unfinished but eager. A puppy about to be house-trained. The edges of his ears are red, probably because he's just been pulling at them. One more bad habit his bride is going to sort out for him. It's clear from the way the camera focuses on her that she's the one in control.

You're supposed to look at your wedding photographs once a week. It keeps your marriage alive. I skip them a bit though, if I'm honest, and turn to the babies. I tell the seasons of the passing years through these photographs. Naked bodies in the paddling pool come summer; witches and goblins in the autumn, faces pressed up at windows to watch fireworks go off in the garden; mittened hands throwing snowballs; chocolate smeared Christmas mornings; wellington boots nudging the first snowdrops; fingers clutching nursery pictures of daffodils; and back to bodies in the paddling pool. Brightly patterned swimsuits and better artwork the only indication of time moving on.

And smiles are the one constant. I'm sure it's the main reason I look through this box of photographs so often. There don't seem to be too many smiles in our house these days.

*

We've just finished supper.

At least we can sometimes manage to eat together, even if everyone disappears afterwards. Calum is out every evening with his friends, Emma just spends her time reading in her room and Peter's working. Work, work, work. He thinks if I could only pull myself together everything will be alright.

He wants me to see a doctor. But I won't go. What could any doctor say to me? That I need to go outside? But what will happen to all of us though if I do start leaving the house? What would happen to Peter without me here to look out for him? He hasn't thought of that.

It's nice to be able to visit Mary. I anaesthetise myself with television usually, sipping at wine like on a mother's teat. It turned out to be a good job I'd started to take some furniture down. That's when Mary came to visit me. She called it a little nest I'd made.

Funny she came at that moment. She didn't normally pop in. All that travelling up to London and the swanky job and shopping didn't leave her much time. You're like Peter, I thought when she came in. She had that same air of briskness, of better places to go. Then she came and stood next to me so close and I thought why she even smells like Peter. I felt tongue-tied then, the way I sometimes do with Peter, and I was still a bit dusty from moving the sofa and the table down there and she just stood there looking at me.

"You've made a proper little nest here, haven't you Caroline?" she said. "Planning to hibernate down here and leave the rest of the family?"

And then she laughed. And in that one moment she spoiled everything I'd done in the basement. Because I had been making a nest, although I didn't call it that. A room of one's own, I thought. But I didn't say that because I couldn't bear her to look surprised at the fact that I'd been reading Virginia Woolf. That patronising little face she made every time she spoke to me. And then she asked me if I could pick up her kids and give them supper. Something had come up, she said.

"It's hard to think of anyone else to ask," she said. "After all, you're hardly going anywhere are you? And –"

And then the phone rang and it was Peter. You're going to be working late, I said before he had the chance to say anything. He stumbled then, started making excuses but I stopped him dead. It's the lies you get the most tired of.

Mary must have been listening because when I came back she was all alert as if her nerve ends were standing up all over her skin. Knife-edge. She tried to pretend everything was OK but I knew it was what she'd come to hear. It was the way she asked about it, so eager. Her mouth was almost watering.

"Was that Peter? Nothing wrong I hope," she asked.

That's when I realised she'd come to gloat. Everyone think she's so nice. So enterprising to hold down such a big job and keep everything together especially when her husband's got that little drink problem we can't talk about because it'll mean that Mary's not perfect. But at that moment I saw her getting such pleasure at the thought of asking her lover's wife to look after her kids so the two of them could meet. She loved the cruelty of it. I could picture her and Peter laughing about it.

I had to shut the door then and lock it behind me I was so angry. It was a way of protecting her but of course she wouldn't see it like that.

I went back when she started screaming. Told her that it was like fighting with a sister. I always used to dream I was a twin. Thought that one day I'd find that other half who thought and acted the same way as me.

Mary and I could look alike. Especially when she doesn't wear make-up and her hair's all over the place. She's going to have to watch out for that. I'm going to move a mirror down into the cellar and we can make a list of all the things she needs.

*

I went out today.

Not far, but out. I went to the shops and got things. Lipstick, make-up, that sort of thing. Little things but it's a start. I ran back, pushing over people in my hurry to get back inside my

92

door, but there was no harm done. Everything was as it was before except I'd been out.

Emma noticed. She told me I looked better. That I reminded her of someone but she couldn't think who.

Adventure, that's the name of this lipstick. How could I
resist that? There was even one called Dangerous Liaisons. I'm
wearing fudge on my eyes and adventure on my lips. Sugar and
spice.

"What we're both made of," I told Mary.

*

I sit up here more and more now I can't spend all my time
downstairs. Not now with Mary in the cellar. The two of us need
some space sometimes, otherwise our relationship can become a
bit intense.

The good news is that I've been going out more. And
I've started to write this journal. I chose it because of this beautiful green colour. I take it upstairs and write about my day. Once
you start, there's so much to say. You have no idea. I read it to
Mary every evening. I think she likes it. We're teaching each
other.

I go and see her husband too. He's missing her of course
but she was supposed to be in China. She'd arranged her own
childcare and everything for the week and apparently it's quite
normal for Mary's trips to go on longer.

I encouraged him to go out to the pub while I babysat
Rebecca. It was the least I could do. I like being in other people's houses when they're not there anyway, looking in their private places, smelling their smells.

When Simon came back, I agreed with him that it
would be stupid to worry just yet. Things will out, I said. If
there's any funny business going on then you'll find clues. There
are always clues.

Imagine going to China. But when I asked Mary what it was like, she had nothing to say. It's wasted. I walk down the street on the other hand and I've got stories coming out of my ears. Do you know the other day I saw a dog walking along holding its lead in its mouth. And just yesterday in the supermarket, the man behind me had twenty white sliced loaves and twelve jars of strawberry jam in his shopping trolley. Why did he need so many? What was his story? It's just a question of looking.

It's no wonder I'm too busy to go through the photographs so often. They've become a treat, not a necessity.

See this one of Calum. He's covered with chocolate mousse, even the tops of his ears. It was Christmas Day and he hadn't liked the lunch so I gave him that. Peter's mother was there. She said that when Peter was small if he didn't eat lunch, she'd put it in the fridge and bring it out again and again until he did eat it up. It hasn't harmed him, she said, and I had to say no. But I did wonder afterwards.

That's why I don't say anything to Mary when she won't eat her meals up. I just take the tray away. I'm spending a lot of time cooking now to try and find things she'll like. The funny thing is that it's going down well with the rest of the family. For years and years, I toiled to please them. Now that it's not them I'm trying to tempt, they're falling at my feet.

*

I had a difficult chat with Mary today. I had to tell her that she wasn't the first for Peter. I knew he'd manage to persuade her that she was. Probably told her that it was true love, but the others thought the same too. There's something about secret love that needs to be told, isn't there? And who better to tell but the wife. I've got used to the phone calls, although funnily enough it's the ones that don't say anything that worry me the most. It's as if they just want to hear the air around Peter. You can hear them breathing in so deeply and I need to put the phone down quickly then before they breathe out because it's as if their desperation has the power to pollute the atmosphere even through the receiver.

I've taken to using all these scented candles, all the incense sticks. They mask the smell of pain. Of failure. Even the fairy lights add drops of sparkle that light up the dark corners.

Where was I? Peter. He likes my hair like this. Thinks the dark brown a bit severe but says I remind him of Lois Lane. I got on top of him in bed the other night and called him Superman. He loved that. We've never played games before. I think it surprised him. He says he never knows what he's going to find when he comes home these days. I've got Mary to thank for that. I thought I'd go shopping for both of us tomorrow. Buy us some new clothes. Something daring, the kind of thing I've never dared wear before. Something that will suit both of us.

*

Emma came back from school today saying Rebecca had been sent home. Apparently she hit Dmitri because he said her mother was a slut. He said that Rebecca's Dad had told his Dad that he'd found all sorts of things in Rebecca's Mum's cupboards.

Emma said that everyone knew that Rebecca's Mum had run off with another man. Emma said she was pleased to have a Mum like me. Not one like Mary. It made me want to cry when she said how different we were. I went downstairs afterwards and had another look at Mary.

*

Let me just light the candles. These ones are lavender. I love the smell of lavender. It reminds me of the holidays in Provence we used to go before we had kids. Peter and I used to cycle for days and days, eating picnics under olive trees and making love in the long grass. Our bodies got so toned and brown. Each night we could count every new muscle indentation, running our fingers up and down each other's legs like ants.

I've been writing about that in my journal. Trying to remember the past for what it was, not for how the present has made it. Dan says I've got a talent. Haven't I told you about Dan? He's the writing teacher for the group at the library. That's where I am every Thursday morning now. I've been writing short stories, poems, a play even. Dan says he's going to help me get published. Imagine me − a writer. Dan and I go to the pub after class. He's quite different from Peter who has never seen my depth.

*

I went to see Mary's husband again this evening. He'd been drinking, of course. Told me everything he'd told the police. About the letters he'd found in Mary's cupboards. Copies of letters she'd sent to the man, calling herself his mistress. Apparently she wrote that just saying it sounded French and sexy. Reminded her of silk stockings and bruises.

He must have found them just after my last visit because he didn't mention them before. He'd no idea Mary was having an affair when she left. That's why he didn't tell the police anything at the time. He said the police were disappointed there was nothing from the man, but as he pointed out she'd hardly be writing to herself, would she?

I baby-sat Rebecca for a couple of hours when Simon went to the pub. I got Rebecca to show me their photograph albums. I like to fill in the gap with photos. Gives me ideas for my novel. My novel. I like the sound of that. Dan says − I have told you about Dan, haven't I? − he says that I'm a born writer. That my imagination sparkles. Fancy me sparkling. Although I can't walk down the street these days without someone shouting out at me. I feel as if I'm on heat. Sometimes I think this is what it must be like to be other women. What it must be like to be Mary.

I can't tell Peter. That's the only sad thing about it. He's so down in the dumps these days. Positively un-sparkling. And he's always at home, hanging around me. It's like Mary said in her letter to him. Now what did she say – oh yes, *breathing the same air, occupying the same space as you is like a dream I don't think I'll ever be lucky enough to achieve.*

Nice words. I'd be proud to write something like that. Maybe that's why I suggested Mary's husband took those letters down to the pub with him. It's not your shame, I said. It's hers. I told him he should talk to as many people as he could about it. Tell everyone what he really felt. And so what if he sounded a bit mad. Everyone will understand, I said.

People don't realise how powerful the written word can be. Dan says that the mere act of writing things down is a kind of prophecy. A way of controlling the future. You see, in any relationship there's one partner who wants to bear witness and one who wants the whole thing to be a story that's written on the wind. Dan says that I'll need to write about Peter's betrayals. This is the only way I'm going to take back the power he has over me. You have to use words as your sword, he says. Write your way out of your own situation. You have to be prepared to take control, even if it's difficult.

It was the same advice I told Mary when I said goodbye to her. Didn't I tell you she left? I was sad to see her go, but we'd both run out of things to teach each other. And now I'm so busy I couldn't really give her the attention she deserved.

"We're different people now, Mary," I said, "than when you first came here."

She's going somewhere quiet, Mary. Somewhere she won't be found. I suppose you can say she's escaped the everyday. It's hard not to feel jealous of her in many ways.

*

You'll never guess what has happened. Simon has been arrested for Mary's murder. And they've not even found a body. They published Mary's letters in the local newspaper. The whole neighbourhood is divided. Half think that Mary has run away with her fancy man and the other half believe that Simon has really killed her and wrote the letters himself as a decoy. The only thing they're all agreed on is that both are as bad as each other. Everyone feels cheated at how they were taken in by thinking they were both so perfect.

It's hard on us all. You think you know someone, you think you've tested every limit they have, you think there's nothing they could do to surprise you, and they turn round and do something like commit a murder. There's always more to people than you imagine, isn't there? That Jekyll and Hyde quality of danger that keeps you guessing.

The trouble is that most of us don't bother to look for challenges. We live our lives on the bottom level and never reach up to our true potential. What we could do if pushed. Oh, not just murder, but art too. Dan says it comes from the same fire. You just need to keep stoking it.

Of course with some people you keep hoping. They say it's the quiet ones that are always the worst, the ones like Peter. But you keep scratching the surface expecting something hot and you find a spreadsheet, a business report. That lover's assignation you imagine every second of turns out to be a genuine late meeting. There's no heart there although you keep wishing, keep hoping. You wonder if things could be different – if you could be different – would you see another side then? Is it your fault? It's part of the attraction, that hidden side. He can't help it, Peter. He doesn't even know himself what he's doing. The effect he has on women. I have to watch that. Be the ones to take the risks for him.

Take obsession for instance. What would you write to someone you're obsessed with? *Breathing the same air, occupying the same space is like a dream I don't think I'll ever be lucky enough to achieve.* It makes me think of an exercise Dan set us in class one day, not long after Mary had disappeared. When I first started leaving the house. He asked us to think of a letter that would drive someone else to murder. Most of the group did the usual – letters from bank managers announcing overdrafts, from teenagers to mothers, parents to sons. But I put myself in Mary's shoes. How would she react if she was in love with someone as unlikely as, as unlikely as my Peter for instance. Dan thought my letter was wonderful. He said it was as if I'd lived in Mary's mind for months, imagining, wondering, sensing what might have been going on between the two of them.

"Such passion," he said and I didn't move then when he leant over me to correct my writing. Not an inch.

"I want more," he said, and I looked at him properly then.

"I'm married," I said. "I live for my husband. Just because he never says so doesn't mean I don't know how much he needs me."

Dan came to see me the day the whole thing appeared in the papers. He wanted to talk about the letters but I told him I had nothing more to give him. He was a good teacher but I think in the end I proved a better pupil. I'm still surprised at how much I miss him. But then I think of Peter. One of us needs to keep our focus, and I've been going out too much lately.

This is the last time I'm going to be coming down here. There's something a bit morbid about it. I need light, dust sparkling in the sun through an open window. I've put a desk upstairs in the sitting room. Peter complained a bit but I just asked him when was the last time he'd sat there. He took my point. I've cleared up all those old photographs, put them upstairs in the loft. I hadn't been up to the loft for a long time. It was surprisingly comfortable. I took a chair up there as well and some cushions.

Susan, Josie's mother, called round when I was in the middle of it.

"What a pretty little nest you've made up here," she said and I just smiled. She didn't think I'd noticed the snapshot of Peter she stole and hid in her coat pocket.

Keeping the Rules

I want to tell you a story. Not to explain myself or to make you feel sorry for me. It happened too long ago for all that. Such a long time ago, when I was a small boy.

So why am I telling you now? I thought you'd be pleased. It's the sort of thing you keep telling me we should share. I can't promise it's going to be easy, but you see, I honestly couldn't think how I could make you understand and then I suddenly thought, why not try it Francesca's way? Why not let it out, spill the beans, rake over the past? Why not join her in an orgy of memory and confession?

Don't worry, I'm not drunk. Yet.

Come and sit here, on the sofa and let me take your shoes off. Don't shiver when I touch you. Anyone would think you were scared of me. I'm going to put your feet here so you can lie right down. Rest your head against the cushion and I'll arrange your hair so it frames your face. Now keep looking up at the ceiling. Don't move. I keep forgetting how young you are. Sometimes you look more like my child than my wife.

Perhaps we should play a game. Would that make you feel more relaxed? Imagine you're lying on your back on a beach, watching the stars. And then if I go over to the other side of the room, take this wooden chair and turn it round so it faces the wall, I'm going to pretend you're not there. Let me fill my glass first. Don't say anything. I don't need a nurse tonight. Tonight, I'm the one in charge.

No, don't look at me. I'll keep my back to you while I
tell this story and you can lie there like a small child being read
to by its mother. Didn't your mother ever tell you bedtime stories? Of course she did. You were one of the lucky ones. She
filled you up with once upon a time's and happily ever after's
until you had no space left for real stories. Well, this is mine.
Treat it as a gift. Are you comfortable? Good, then I'll begin.

It happened in my first year at boarding school. I must
have been about nine the first time the housemaster called me
into his study. I can remember it clearly. It was a rainy Sunday
afternoon. We had a gap of a few hours between Church and
tea that was the only bit of the week we could call our own. It
used to be as if time moved differently then. I would stand at the
corners of empty corridors and listen out for the voices of other
boys; boys from the past or the future. It didn't matter which so
long as I was free - for a few minutes - from the present.

I thought he wanted to discuss my crying. I'd got into
the habit of waking up half an hour earlier than anyone else and
creeping downstairs to the common room. I'd sit completely
straight in one of the lumpy armchairs, fingering the flowery
rough material of the arm cape and when I was ready, I'd cry.
You'll probably laugh but I'd developed this technique which
allowed me to master my tears completely. First of all, I'd count
to fifty, very slowly, so as to prove who exactly was in control
and then, only when I decided it was time would I let them flow
silently down my cheeks. But what made me really proud was
the way I could stop dead at any minute. Usually when I heard
the first footstep on the stairs. We all shared the pack mentality.
Had breakfast at the same time, did everything at the same time,
so one person getting up meant everyone else was coming too.
By the time anyone came into the room, I'd have wiped away
the evidence and would be energetically browsing the bookcases,
springing from one ball of my foot to the other in the way we all
did, like tennis players.

I should have known I couldn't keep it a secret. If privacy was not actively discouraged then it was certainly something to be suspicious of. After all, the only reason you could have for being private was that you were doing something you shouldn't be doing. I couldn't argue with this. You didn't reach my age without knowing that boys didn't cry.

I'll keep the bottle over here now. This story needs some lubrication and then I won't have to keep disturbing you. It's funny how it all comes back. It must have been more than 40 years ago. Longer than you've been alive, 'Cesca.

I knocked on the master's door firmly, looking up and down the corridor first to see if anyone was there. It was empty apart from the crooked line of photographs of cricket and rugby teams. So many boys eager to be captured doing the right thing, sitting hands on knees, all staring the camera straight in the eye. The faces betrayed the same hope throughout the years; the only way you could tell the era was whether they were in black and white or colour.

"Come in," he barked and I swung the door open, stepping inside and clicking my heels together as if I was saluting.

"You wanted to see me, Mr Martin," I said in my brightest voice. This is the way we were encouraged to be. Like miniature soldiers.

There were three rules we learnt early on. Number one - always do whatever a master says, no questions asked. Number two - keep cheerful whatever the world throws at you. Number three - never, ever, show your vulnerability. Except we didn't put it quite like that. We'd call it being wet or drippy and make mock puking noises in the background. Number three was the most important rule and this is where I thought I'd been caught out, you see.

"Ah yes, Armstrong." His desk was crowded high with piles of papers so he had to peer over the top of them to see me. He wheeled himself round in his wooden office chair, presenting his profile to me and held up a sheet of blue writing paper in a pincer movement between his thumb and finger. He read the black handwriting for a few seconds and then looked at me.

"Robert. Good, good, come in. Sit down." He smiled then, but I didn't feel reassured. I sat on the edge of the leather armchair opposite him to watch and wait. "Good," he repeated, rubbing his hands together as if he were warming them in front of the fire. "Getting on alright?"

"Yes sir." I tried to project all the confidence I could in those two words, looking not at him but at the bristly tight moustache above his mouth. It stuck out at a 45 degree angle from his skin, forming a canopy for his lips. I suddenly realised he must cut it every day to keep it so sharp. It seemed an odd touch of vanity when the rest of him looked so shabby.

"Lots of friends?"

I nodded but said nothing. It wasn't a direct lie. If I didn't have friends, at least I didn't have enemies. Wasn't one of the bullied boys although there was always the danger. I wonder now if fear didn't lurk in the pits of all our stomachs. Every time I think about school I get these flashbacks to how it felt to have someone perpetually at your back, about to jump on you and bring you down. It was like living in the middle of a rugby scrum. I know it's no justification but you have to see that's why I push you away sometimes. Why space is so important to me.

No, please don't interrupt. This is my story. It won't take much longer.

"This is hard, hard," he said and collapsed into the chair next to me, his long legs spread out. He was a gangly man and I remember he had one of those Adam's apples that was always bobbing up and down his chicken skin neck. He had all these strange mannerisms, constantly trying to flatten down his hair at the front, for instance, or thrusting his chin out. His worst one was to pinch his nostrils whenever he sneezed.

Perhaps it was to hide my disgust when he leant into me that I tried to look sympathetic. I was just wishing he'd get on with it. I'd heard about his punishments already. Apparently, the worst thing was the way he would cry afterwards. Rawlings even said he'd felt the master's tears dripping onto his back right in the middle of his caning. It was the sort of thing that made you lose respect for someone. That was probably why Martin's set words at these times had become such a joke in the dormitory. Before one of us inflicted any pain on another we would chant them. "This is harder for me than it is for you." You both had to laugh then - tormentor and victim - otherwise you weren't showing the correct spirit.

"I've had a letter from your mother," Martin was saying. "She wanted me to speak to you."

I looked down at my feet, checking the laces were showing the exact same length from the knot. She probably would be upset. My father had told me that my mother wasn't a strong woman. He'd even said that it was our duty as men to protect her from the rest of the world. And although I couldn't understand why it had been her they'd contacted about the tears, secretly I was pleased. I can remember thinking that it might be the one thing that could draw us closer. Do you know, Francesca, I think I even thought the two of us might sit at home weeping each morning before I saw how impractical that would be. My father would never allow it.

"You see, er Robert, your mother is, well, let's just say she's distraught."

Martin's voice floated over me, bursting my dream bubble. I knew what was coming next. My mother often went away when things got too bad. I haven't told you this before, but she was away even when she died. It wasn't something we ever mentioned, but I suppose it was some kind of rest home she went to.

"Look at me, boy."

I jerked my head up. Although I was shocked by the sudden change in his tone, it was so much more familiar to me than his forced camaraderie that it was almost welcome.

"It's about your father. I understand he's not been well for some time and that you knew this. But now, you see, your

106

mother has asked me to tell you that your father is, well, your father, there's no easy way to tell you this but, you see, Robert, your father has died."

I looked at him, watching the way his eyes - blue, a very watery pale blue, I think they were - bulged out of their sockets. I used to have a pet rabbit with eyes like that. A friend had once told me that if you squeezed the neck long and hard enough, those sort of eyes would pop out and dangle on the end of a piece of sinew curling round and round like string. I was worried that if the master's eyes fell out, I would have to push them back into the sockets with my fingers. I could even hear the noise they would make when they were sucked back into place - squirrsssshhh.

I was told later that my vomit covered the wall behind Martin so completely that when he moved, the outline of his figure was clearly shown against the contrast of the clean wall-paper. It was something I'd have liked to have seen, but I was never able to find anyone who had actually been in the study before it was cleaned up. Many of the boys did say that for days afterwards Martin rubbed his moustache constantly as if he'd got something nasty stuck there. You're probably feeling disgusted, but I'd become a hero by this time. Even the senior boys had got to know my name.

When I woke up, I was in the sickroom. Matron was sitting beside my bed, sewing. I tried to scrunch up my eyes just wide enough so I could watch her without her noticing. It made me feel oddly powerful but I knew the minute she realised I'd come to, she'd be the one in control. It was so peaceful lying there, in a pool of cool, clean white. Everything was white - the walls, the floor, the bed, blankets, sheets, matron's uniform, even her hair. It was as if I was on a cloud, no longer linked to the world. I can remember it vividly. It was such a good feeling.

I had to go back to the master's room one more time. I thought he looked at me warily and I was aware of swaggering a little. I sniffed the room surreptitiously but all I could smell was furniture polish and air freshener.

"Everything alright?" he asked and I nodded. "Have you written to your mother?"

I nodded again.

"That's good. You're the man of the family now. The one they'll all be relying on."

I tried to look as if I could take it, standing up straight and tall.

"Right. Good. Well, I expect you've got things to do now. Just wanted to make sure everything was fine."

I paused for a moment. I wanted to ask him where my mother was. My aunt had come to tell me about my father in person. We'd had an uncomfortable tea together at the one smart hotel in the small town near the school. I think she probably chose it so I wouldn't be tempted to break down. Even at nine, I was aware she had no patience for what she called my mother's hysterics. She told me that my father's death had been for the best and asked whether I wanted another piece of cake. Any mention of my mother just got her angry and all she would say was that it was better for me not to see her. That everything was for the best. I noticed her staring at me in a funny way after that, as if I was getting hysterical too, so I just smiled back at her and took the cake. Fruit cake always sticks in my throat. Even now.

I was trying to judge whether it was safe to ask Martin about my mother when he laughed, an odd uncomfortable bark which nevertheless broke the tension. "Good," he said, cracking his knuckles, so I smiled too trying to make it clear I was as keen and eager to get back into the scrum as he was to get rid of me. But when I left his room, I just stood in the corridor, my back against the wall, thousands of tiny faces staring out at me. You see, the awful thing was I couldn't stop my knees from shaking. I knew I'd collapse if I tried to walk.

I must have stayed there for about ten minutes. When I regained control, I went straight into the common room downstairs. All the other boys were there, watching television. I stood in the doorway for a few seconds, peering into the gloom. Then, choosing my moment, just when the music was building up into a crescendo of tension, I let out an enormous cry and dived over the back of the sofa, screaming, lashing out with my wrists and feet, rolling over and over until I was at the bottom of a heap of writhing bodies. I wasn't sure which desire was strongest - to hurt or to be hurt. I wanted the lights out, to be taken over by the blackness.

Five of us had to go and see the master. He looked surprised to see me amongst the troublemakers but at least he didn't pick me out for special treatment. I can remember giggling when he actually said the words the first time. "This is harder for me..."

"...than it is for you," I whispered to the next in line.

Why that little gasp? Being hit is nothing. With any punishment, it is the spirit of the thing that matters. He wasn't hurting us to give himself pleasure but because it was what you did to teach someone a lesson they would benefit from. The important thing was that we understood that. It was part of the rules. What still impresses me is the way we had to stand up straight and say thank you afterwards. It was that attention to detail that ensured you kept your dignity, a modicum of control in the situation.

Don't worry. I'm not going to start another lecture about the importance of backbone and discipline. We know each other's views on that one, but let me just say it is one of the few things that makes me glad we never had any joy in the baby department.

Ah. Now I have got your attention. I can feel you sit up, staring at me. Please don't move just yet. This is hard enough as it is.

Why can't you see it's too late for me? You knew my
feelings when you married me. I made no false promises. You
say now that you were too young to know what it would feel like,
the bone-numbing sadness of never being a mother, but I don't
believe that. You're too strong to need anyone else to complete
you. Unlike me. Don't you see how weak I am compared to
you?

Let me tell you about that night in the dormitory, lying
there awake. I was nine years old and that night, after the second chat, my first caning, I couldn't shut my eyes for worrying
about how I would have to leave school and start working to
support my mother. Everyone kept on at me, telling me that I
was the man of the house. Even my father had drummed it into
me that it was my job to look after my mother. I pictured him in
his suit and glasses, sitting on a white fluffy cloud, looking down
at me in my narrow bed and expecting me to do the right thing.

You can never imagine how I felt. I wanted to scream
that I was still a child. That I'd never had a chance to enjoy my
childhood. And that was the first time it really sank in that I
didn't have anyone I could talk to. Not one person who would
have listened to me.

I knew that would get you. Bring you over to me. That's
it. Put your arms tight around my back but I'm not going to look
at you yet. I've not finished, you see. Fill my glass up one last
time and I'll tell you what else came out of the whole thing. You
remember my crying. My morning tears. When I went down the
next morning to have my usual weep, I found I had lost control.
I couldn't get the tears to flow at all. I thought about every sad
thing I could but nothing worked. My body simply refused to do
what it was told.

I sat there, dry-eyed, in that chair and all I could feel
was an overwhelming relief. It was wonderful not to have this
secret any more. I can remember skipping to breakfast along
with anyone else that morning and for the first time, perhaps the
first time in my life, I felt normal.

Sshhh. Don't spoil things. I know it wasn't what you might call normal but it was enough for me. I don't think I've ever dared to ask for as much as you do from life. You say I've cut off all my emotions but I can't be careless like you, dropping love here and there in great dollops, not worrying about the returns. The joke of it all, the last laugh, is the strength this gives you. I have to keep constantly on guard whereas you'll win every battle simply because you can afford to lose.

Take now. You don't know what you do to me when you hold me like this. Let me turn round, put my face against your breast. That's it. I can hear your mouth humming just above my ear. Rock me gently, so gently. It's so safe here, just the two of us. So safe.

Maggots in the Rice

She's in Ghuanzou, Southern China and it's hot. So hot. Her cotton skirt is sticking to her legs and she can feel a trail of sweat trickling down her back. She has to keep one hand permanently up to lift the hair off her nape, and that's with the air-conditioning.

Standing on the first floor balcony of her luxury Western-style hotel, she can look right into the atrium below. It must be some special children's festival because there are kids everywhere. She watches the families taking photos of themselves against the backdrop of the massive waterfall that cascades down the marble foyer.

"Maggots in the rice." An American voice breaks into her contemplation. The man standing next to her makes the statement in a conversational tone, as if she had just asked the time.

"Sorry?" She's heard the expression before. It's what the Chinese are supposed to call unwanted girl babies, but she doesn't understand why he's said it.

"Maggots in the rice," he repeats. "You look down there and tell me what sex those children are."

"Girls." All girls. It's odd she hadn't noticed before. She prides herself on being observant.

"Yeah, and do the parents look sad?" She shakes her head. They don't. They are laughing as they pay homage to their daughters. Daughters who exaggerate the feminine with their many petticoated frocks, large hair bows and imperious expressions.

"We go around saying the Chinese think it is a disaster to have a daughter, but for these guys, it is just one more thing to show off about." He puts on a bad Chinese accent. "I no need boy to look after me in old age. I have plenty money spend on girl."

She nods. She hadn't thought about it that way before. Below them the families are shouting at each other in the Chinese way that still gets her jangly. They manage to make even a friendly instruction for a grandfather to smile at the camera sound like a call for a firing squad. Short, staccato sounds fill the air, and watching the bustle she can't get rid of the image of birds in a feeding frenzy.

Because she's looking down, she's aware of watching the scene as if these are not real people but then she's hit by a shock of pain when a small girl flings her arms around her mother's neck. She can't remember the last time her own daughter Lara hugged her like that, so lovingly.

"Do you have children?" she asks. It doesn't seem too personal a question. She's had her most intimate conversations with strangers she's met abroad. There is something about speaking the same language that breaks down the barriers..

"Naa, never had time. I'm Jim Lennox by the way," he holds out his hand. "I've seen you before, with the English party. The teachers."

"Rachel Stevens." She shakes his hand formally, wincing as he squeezes hers too tight. She's not small, but Jim Lennox towers over her. He is broad too. In good shape although he looks as if he works hard at it. Despite the traditional appearance of his clothes, blue blazer and jeans, they are all too neat, too tailored. She's often noticed that trait before in men who have spent a long time in the East.

They spend the next few minutes making small talk, agreeing that the hotel is very comfortable, China is very hot and the children are very noisy. Noisy but sweet, she says, throwing back her head so her hair swings round over shoulders, catching his eye and holding the gaze for a second more than necessary. Then, when she sees an answering glint, she turns back to watch the families below.

It's part instinct, part boredom. It's only afterwards that she'll analyse how she feels and whether it was worth it. At the moment, it's the thrill of the chase she's after; the chance to be part of something - or someone - else for just a while. Where's the harm? She's giving as well as taking.

Jim comes to stand close to her. When she feels his body touch hers, she doesn't move. That's the bit that can be difficult.

"How did you know they were teachers?" she asks, flashing him a look out of the corner of her eye. It is almost disappointing in the way it never fails.

"I asked," he replies unashamedly. "I suppose they're here to drum up custom for those miserable schools of theirs."

"It's a wonderful opportunity for these children." They both know she's lying, but he just shrugs. She travels all over the East organising meetings between English boarding schools and prospective Asian parents. It's a lucrative business and when she's in danger of being shocked by what she sees - the five-year-olds being sent to the other side of the world; the ten-year-olds who carry out all the negotiations for nodding, smiling parents - she reminds herself that she's paid by commission.

"So how many of these little kids have you signed up?" Jim asks, waving his hand down at the crowded foyer. It is hard to tell in the East, but the Rolex on his wrist looks real.

"Not too many this time," she says. "The money's here but the paperwork's a problem."

"What you need is a good lawyer who knows the system. I'll give you my card."

She takes it, running her finger around the gold edges. He's based in Bangkok, and she has no immediate plans to go to Thailand. This is a good thing. You don't always want to keep running into the same people.

"Tell me about it over a drink," she says.

Jim goes on ahead down the hotel's white marble staircase but Rachel takes her time, running her hand along the smooth banister. When she reaches the bottom, Jim is standing by the waterfall with his arm around a waitress. He turns towards Rachel and holds out his hand.

"My good friend here is about to get us a table," he explains so laboriously that she can tell it's more for the waitress's benefit than hers.

The girl bows, giggling. "This way," she says and walks straight through the sheet water of the waterfall. The families carry on milling around taking their photographs as if nothing has happened.

"Come on. Don't tell me you're scared." Jim is holding Rachel's hand so she is forced to follow.

"This is a silk blouse," she says. "You'll ruin it."

But there's a hidden passage. They walk hand in hand a few steps in the dark until, completely dry, they enter a stone grotto lit by streamers of fairy lights which throw off a glittery reflection on the wavy wall of water. Despite the ubiquitous air conditioning, it is the first time in China Rachel has felt naturally cool.

The waitress is lugging over a heavy table and two chairs while Jim just stands by, not offering to help. Rachel thinks about nudging him but then decides it's none of her business. When the table is set up, the girl turns to Jim. "Champagne?" she asks, and Rachel can see she's flirting. She looks at Jim again. He could be quite handsome, she thinks, if you ignore the lapses of taste - the monogrammed shirt pocket, the snakeskin belt, the slip on shoes. Small shoes. She's never forgotten what they used to say about men with small feet at school.

Jim's surprisingly easy to talk to. Or maybe it is the magic of that little grotto. Every so often, Rachel pauses to rest her head on the back of the chair, luxuriating in the light drops of water that fall onto her face.

She tells Jim her life story and the disappointment she feels that her marriage is going nowhere. "He complains I'm always away but he never stops to think about how much money I'm earning. If it wasn't for my daughter I'd leave, but I think she deserves a father," she says, "however pathetic." But when she laughs, Jim doesn't. He takes up her hand and strokes it very gently with his fingertips until she thinks she might cry.

To change the atmosphere, she starts to tell him about the others in the group. She's proud of her reputation as an amusing story teller and throws herself into making Jim laugh, mimicking an elderly headmaster one minute; the inexperienced deputy who's out of his depth the next. But even as she's talking, she knows it's wasted. Jim's not even smiling.

"Why do you do this job if you hate it so much?" he asks.

She doesn't know what to say. She'd only been trying to make conversation. "We all have to do things we don't like sometimes," she says. "There's no need to get on your high horse."

He laughs and shields his head with his hands as if to ward off an attack. "How long is an average trip - three weeks?" he asks. "It's a long time to be away from your daughter."

"She's fine. I always bring her something nice back. It's not 'Oh Mummy, how nice to see you' but 'where's my present?' Children are mercenary like that."

"Is she an only child?"

"Yes. We never intended to have any kids, but accidents happen. I swore I'd never go through another pregnancy although if Dave had his way, I think he'd have a houseful by now. I'm not really the maternal type."

Jim laughs loudly. "I'd never have guessed," he says and she smiles back at him. "What does your husband do?" he asks.

Rachel finds it hard to work out what men mean when they ask this question. In some cases, it's a sign they're definitely interested; that they're assessing the competition. At other times, it's a way of drawing the situation to a close. She sometimes thinks that by bringing in Dave, they feel they are handing her back to him, their honour intact. Either way, it's a bore. She doesn't care about their wives.

"He's in computers," she says, looking straight at Jim, showing him she's got nothing to hide. She learnt early on that there was no point making any excuses or justifications for her behaviour.

"So while the mouse is away, she plays." He's smiling and she laughs, although it's not that good a joke. She just wants to show that she's on his side; that she's not playing games.

"Don't you ever get caught out?" he asks. "You don't know anything about me after all. No-one knows where you are or who you're with."

"The waitress does," she says.

"Yes, but she's my accomplice. I pay her to help me lure women in here." He's still smiling but Rachel shivers. She doesn't understand where this conversation is leading. She thought they were both clear about what they wanted.

On the other side of the water, the noise of the children has turned to crying, even to screams. They're tired, she thinks automatically. She knows herself from taking Lara out that treats normally do end in tears. Nothing can quite live up to the excitement of how wonderful it was all going to be. She listens for the sound of parents placating their children but all she can hear is harsh shouting. It makes her head ache and she wishes, not for the first time, that she had married a stronger man, one who would stop her getting into situations like this.

She's aware that Jim Lennox is watching her but when she puts her hand up to check her hair, it's damp from the water.

She forces herself to smile at Jim, and catches him taking a quick look at his watch. "Let's go," he says.

She pauses for a few seconds, pretending to watch the waterfall, but then he reaches across and gently strokes a lock of her hair away from her face, tucking it behind her ear. "Shall we go?" he asks, holding out his hand.

Rachel nods and puts her hand in his, still not looking at him.

Leading the Dance

Deborah has ruined his life. It's important that she knows this. Does she know what it feels like for a man to have someone chipping away at his very being? Does she know? Does she? It's no wonder he gets angry at them all. He can't help it. It's not his fault.

He doesn't often hit out, but then he doesn't have to. A look, a word and they get the message. They're well trained. They walk carefully, don't make any noise, don't get in the way. For a child to cry during one of Daddy's moods is not a good thing because then he'll teach them how it really feels to hurt.

They all act, but he's the best at it. He's the smiling matchstick man on Father's Day cards, the clown at birthday parties, the cheque-signer on shopping sprees. They're so lucky to have a man like him. So lucky.

(The more Deborah says 'lucky' the odder it becomes. Words are like that. They let you down when you need them most. 'Friend' is another one. See how ugly it is when you really look at it. The letters aren't easy together. It doesn't feel right in the mouth either. It twists the jaw, gets stuck in the back of the throat so you gag. Better to stick to words that get straight to the point. Words like 'strike'. You spit it out before you know what you are doing. You can't help it. It's not your fault.)

120

It's the fact that she's expecting him to go to a school ceilidh that's the problem. For him. To go to a dance. At the School. Doesn't she realise he's made for better things? Doesn't she feel guilty she's dragged him down to this level? But then she doesn't want to go to the dance either. Not with him. He'll be the life and soul, everyone will want to dance with him, he'll whirl the children round too fast, get them too excited and then they'll all go home together. Alone.

She can't even dance. She'll try to lead the way she always does. This is another of her problems. She's incapable of letting herself go with him. If only she would. If only she would do things the way he says then everything would be alright. Why does she always have to fight? Why can't she try to follow him just once? Will she try? Will she? He supposes he might make the effort to go to the dance. For the children's sake. For Deborah's sake. For the sake of the family. It's only a bloody dance. He used to love to dance.

*

It's at times like this she wishes she had a knife. She can feel its weight in her hand, the ridges in the metal as her fingers cup round the handle. It has to be sharp. Running it along her arm so the point makes ripples in the hairs, she'll finally understand what it means to be on knife-edge.

It's her nerve ends she wants to cut away, the ones on her fingertips, in her pupils, on her tongue, between her legs. She can feel them now. Even now, she's melting. He can always do this to her. He's right. She is pathetic, but oh god oh god the way he kisses. What that man can do with his lips, his tongue, his fingers. No one kisses like him.

*

Deborah's watching him now as he dances round her, deliberately twisting his hips as he passes so the fabric from his kilt brushes against her. A woman at the table starts to clap her hands in time to the music, but Deborah knows it's his feet she's applauding. Clap, clap, clap. Clap, clap, clap. It's a man's dance, a dance for men in skirts. They're all wearing the kilt tonight. They're all bravehearts with a passion. It took an Australian and an Irish film star to show them how good they could look, but they've learnt the lesson well. T-shirts and tartan are the new order of the day, and he's looking the best. And he knows it.

He's standing in front of her, holding out his hand. She's careful not to take it. She accepts it instead. Oh yes, he's taught her the difference. She's passive as she lets her hand lie in his and he rewards her with a bow and then a smile. They walk to the dance floor and stand opposite each other, eyes locked. His mouth is counting - *one, two, three, four* - and then he bows again and she curtseys. The dance begins.

They're cautious to begin with, but then there are others laughing and she catches his eye. He nods his head. It's going to be alright. The music's taking over. They become nothing more than the cogs that feed the machine as she receives first one man and then another, bending down now to twirl a small boy, passing him on to the next in line and then it's their turn. She winces as he twists her wrists too tightly and she's spinning, too fast, too fast, but just in time he stops her, hands her over with a click. She takes each outstretched arm that clamours for hers, refusing none, turning round and round and back to him. Always back to him.

He becomes her safety net as she pounds against him again and again and again. *One, two, three, four* ... The line stretches on for ever and then it's his turn. They're back at the beginning. The clapping echoes in her head and she becomes whatever he wants her to be. She's lost herself as her feet start to

122

stamp, her hands pull together and her head bobs up and down. She aches from smiling.

Eventually the music has to stop and she clutches at him to keep upright. He holds her tight, pulling her head back on to his chest as they walk so she feels like his ventriloquist dummy, treading on his toes. She stands up straight, away from him, hearing the hiss too late. When she turns to take his hand, he won't give it to her the way she gave him hers.

At the table, she's so keen to get back to how they were that she lets him yank her down by the hair on to his knee. He plays with her fingers, beating out the music on her shoulders, joggling her up and down. Deborah sits there, unable to join in adult conversations because he's turned her into a child. This is how he likes her. This is how he's happy.

He's calling her name softly now - Deb..or..rah, Deb..or..rah - whispering so she has to lean back to rest her ear against his mouth. "How could you, Deborah?" It's not the words but his breath blowing over her skin she hears. "How could you do this to me?" She looks at him as he continues beaming round the table, his thick arms crossed over in front of her stomach and she squeezes that thin sliver of steel in her clenched fist.

Everyone's quiet as they watch a blue-faced warrior sitting cross-legged on stage tapping out a lament on African drums. Only the children are still twirling on the dance floor, eyes shut as they bump into each other but then they get too wild. Some start to cry. It's time to take them home anyway, put them to bed, share a whisky and a quiet chat together. It's been a good evening.

They follow the crowd out of the school hall. He is carrying a child with one arm, the other tight around her wrist. She watches the families go and knows there are some who think she's lucky to have a man who touches her so often, holds her so close.

When, finally, it's their turn to go through the door he rubs his face into her hair and she can hear him humming. She listens frantically, trying to make sense of the noises he's making but, too soon, he pushes her out in the evening air and she has to shut her eyes tight against the icy wind that slaps at her face. She will never understand him. He'll tell her later. When they're home. When they're alone.

Family Tree

They look so much alike. They always have done.
The sisters are even ageing in the same way - a few silver strands in their dark hair; a network of fine, feathery lines at the top of the cheeks. Susie's one step ahead though, being three years older. It used to annoy Annie that she would never catch up. These days she's not so bothered.

"I thought Dad was going to break down. He sounded so upset," Susie says.

"He told me to drop everything," Annie says. "That she didn't have long."

"Oh God. Was that what he said? She didn't have long. He told me that she'd want to see me. She wanted to have her family round her."

"But would she have been able to speak?"

"'Spose not, but since when has that stopped him?" Susie asks. "He's always spoken for her, hasn't he? Started everything with 'your mum thinks..'."

"Your mum thinks that skirt is too short."

"Your mum thinks you're not working hard enough."

Your mum thinks you should be nicer to your sister, Annie remembers. He must have said something like that to Susie too, but these are things you can't mention.

"Tell me again what the consultant said," she says instead. "About the tree."

"He said her heart is closing off its supplies." Susie has her eyes shut. "It's like a tree with all its branches spreading outwards. The branches are drying off one by one because the oxygen can't reach them."

"Dying," says Annie without thinking.

"What?" Susie opens her eyes sharply.

"Dying. You said drying. The branches of the tree are dying."

"She won't, will she?" asks Susie

"Not tonight," Annie tries to sound reassuring. "Otherwise Dad would never have sent us home. He wouldn't bring us all the way here and then not let us sit by her at the end."

But as she speaks, Annie's thinking that it was just what her father might do. She can imagine exactly what might have been going through his head. The first moments of panic, the phonecalls and then once they were there, his need to have their mother to himself once more.

"Perhaps we should ring the hospital and find out how she is," Annie says.

"Dad said he'd call if there was any news."

"We can't just sit here and wait."

Annie is sitting drawn up in the armchair, resting her cheek against her knees. She's in the perfect position for keening, she thinks, and rocks just slightly so Susie won't notice. It feels surprisingly restful. She can see it might be comforting.

Eventually, the sisters decide on cards. They've always played a lot of cards as a family. Sevens, cheat, rummy, but they all need more than two people. They take a pack of cards each and set up patience, facing each other across the kitchen table.

Annie looks across and sees Susie has a row of red cards facing upwards. That's often the best way to start because once you turn over some black cards you move faster. She's going well herself. A red queen on a black king and she's got a red ten facing upwards. "If I get this out, Mum'll be fine," she tells herself and turns up a black jack immediately. She works on, eyes moving left to right scanning the pattern until she's nearly out.

She pauses for a moment and sees that Susie is turning over the cards one by one, sightlessly. "Hey," she says without thinking. "You're cheating." Susie looks up and for a split second, Annie knows Susie doesn't recognise her.

"I'm going to bed," Susie says. "I can't bear this."

Annie's torn between wanting to finish her game of patience and going up with Susie. The problem is that there's only one spare bed and they haven't talked yet about who will sleep on it. If Susie goes up now, Annie will be left with the floor.

"I'll come too," she says, sweeping up her cards.

They're just going upstairs when the phone rings. Annie holds the receiver sideways so Susie can listen too. Their father tells them that their mother is sleeping now but they're to come in the morning first thing. Their mother will want to see them then, he says. Susie and Annie look at each other and Annie is horrified by her desire to laugh.

"We'll see you in the morning, Dad," Annie says.

"Take care, Dad," Susie calls.

"Well then," he says. "I suppose I'd better get back."

"Well then," says Annie after she's put down the receiver. "I suppose we'd better get to bed."

Susie smiles. They've always been able to laugh together at their father. Encouraged, Annie asks if she fancies a nightcap. "We'll take it up with us," she says, "Like a midnight feast."

They huddle together in the single bed, drinking whisky. "I always said that my ideal man would be someone I could drink whisky with in bed," says Annie.

Susie gives a shriek. "You're rubbing your feet against mine," she says. "You know I hate that."

"I can't help it. There's not enough room."

"Go on the floor."

"You go on the floor."

Annie gives Susie a push as if she's trying to heave her out of bed but Susie twists round quickly, grabs a pillow and holds it over Annie's face.

"Beg for mercy," she says. "Say the magic words."

Annie can remember them as if it was yesterday. "You're a beautiful princess," she chants. "You are the most wonderful sister in the world."

"That's better." Susie lies back on the bed, clutching the pillow to her chest. "It's too small for us both, isn't it?"

"We could go into their bed," suggests Annie tentatively.

"I think that would be best." It's as if the horseplay has reminded them that Susie is the oldest sister. The one who still gets to make the rules. Annie follows her obediently through to their parents bedroom.

"I can smell her handcream," Annie says, holding the sheet up to her nose.

"She never let us into bed with her, did she?" asks Susie, smelling too. "Other children got to sleep whole nights with their parents but she always told us to go back to our own beds."

"Think of something nice and settle back down," Annie mimics her mother's voice exactly. "What did you used to think of?"

"Men selling apples."

"What?" Annie lifts herself up on one elbow so she can look at her sister.

"I used to think of this candy striped stall - pink and white - and there was this man who had rosy cheeks just like the apples he was selling. He used to give me one because I never had any money. I loved the taste of that apple. What about you?"

Annie can't remember. "Sweets probably or cuddly puppies," she says. "I never knew about your apples." She's aware of sounding peeved but she doesn't like to think of her sister lying in the bed next to hers all those years ago, keeping something like the apple man back from her.

"They still love each other don't they?" Susie's got her eyes shut, her arms crossed on her chest over the sheet.

Annie grunts. "You know, when I was very young I never saw them as separate people," she says. "They were always MumandDad. I used to lie in bed sometimes and wish he'd die so she'd love me more."

"Annie no!" Susie keeps her eyes shut but tighter. Annie knows she's said too much but it's too late. She ploughs on, digging her furrow deeper.

"It was as if they wanted our family to be split into two pairs - Them and Us. But it was never Us, was it? It was always you and me separately. So it was Them and me and it was Them and you. I felt as if I never had anyone.

"And then when I got older, I tried to turn it into something positive," she continues. "I thought if I could find someone like Dad, who would love me just as much, then I could become Them." She's silent now because she doesn't want to say the obvious. That it hasn't happened for either of them.

"I know what you mean." Susie talks very quietly so Annie can only just hear her.

"You felt the same?" she asks and Susie nods, eyes still shut.

"Even now," Annie surges on now she feels she's carrying Susie with her. "Even now, it's as if Mum and Dad are at the hospital together and we're here. They don't really want us."

Susie reaches across and fumbles for Annie's hand. "No, they don't," she says.

"They should never have had children," Annie says.

"No, they shouldn't." Susie squeezes Annie's hand hard.

Annie turns to her sister but Susie has moved onto her side her back is facing Annie. It's a sign from the old days of sharing a bedroom that the talking is over. Annie feels the same frustration with her sister that she felt then.

She tries to go back to sleep but the image of her father sitting alone by that hospital bed keeps coming back to her. She tries to replace it with Susie's apple man and for a moment it's alright but then just as he's about to hand her an apple, the man reaches across and pinches Annie's cheek so hard it hurts. She sits up shocked, rubbing her face and listening to Susie's breathing. As her eyes become accustomed to the blackness, she thinks she can make out a shadow standing in the doorway.

"Cuckoos in the nest," she hears a low voice whisper. She tastes the words in her mouth. Cuckoos in the nest. Where did that come from?

She lies back, her heart thumping so hard she tries to still it by putting her hand, palm flat, on her chest. She thinks she'll be awake all night now but when she opens her eyes, it's morning. Susie is leaning over her.

"Wake up," Susie says. "Mum's better. The hospital sent Dad home last night to get some sleep. We're going to see her today." Susie is looking so happy, radiant almost, that Annie wonders whether their conversation last night was a dream.

"Mum..." Her mouth feels all furry and as her hand reaches across to get her glasses, she knocks over the empty whisky glass. "She's really going to be alright?"

"It looks like it." Susie laughs.

"But what about the tree? The branches falling off and stuff."

"Dad says the consultant says it can sometimes happen. The heart starts to recover on its own. They've got to keep her in for tests, of course."

"Where's Dad?"

"Downstairs. He slept in the spare room last night."

"He didn't mind about us here."

"He's so happy about Mum, I don't think he cares about anything this morning." Susie throws Annie a robe. "Hurry up," she says. "Dad says she'll want us to be there when she wakes up."

"Your mum thinks it's a time for families to be together." Annie tries to pass it off as a joke but really she's trying to recreate the closeness she felt with Susie last night. Either way, it doesn't work. Susie's left the room without saying anything, shutting the door firmly behind her.

When Annie walks into the kitchen, she stops for a moment before reaching down to kiss her father. "It's good news about Mum," she says, taking the seat opposite him. But although she looks closely into his eyes, she can read nothing there except the impatience to get back to their mother. Them and Us, she thinks and looks across to where Susie is standing washing up last night's dishes, her back to both of them. Them and me.

Something in the Water

Jane sat on the edge of the swimming pool, dipping one toe into the water to test the temperature.

She told her husband that she liked to come at this time of the evening because there were always so few people. It wasn't a complete lie; more of a half-truth. Fewer people meant she had more space for the one she had come to see. She spotted Patrick immediately over at the far side, but didn't acknowledge him straight away. They had so little time together that ignoring him had become a precious luxury.

A bored father was standing in the shallow end watching a group of children bob up and down on brightly coloured fish-shaped floats. Two pairs of women were chatting together as they swam lengths in unison. The middle of the pool was given over to the serious swimmers. A man was ploughing up and down the fast lane, putting his face up too often to gasp for breath, churning the water with his arms. Jane watched the other swimmers smile tensely at each other to acknowledge the inconvenience. When he was safely out of the way, she slipped into the water.

She realised she'd been dreading this moment. It was like a sacrifice. The fear was out of all proportion to the action, as if a transformation would have to be effected by the time she got out of the pool. She would give something up through her immersion.

Now she hung on to the metal bar at the end to get her breath back before starting to swim. She took her time, concentrating on building up the structure of the stroke. It was the first chance she'd had all day to stretch her body. She reached the other end and floated on her back, her arms bent behind her grasping the bar, her legs scissoring slowly through the water. When Patrick came up, she made her face blank.

"Is everything alright?" he asked and she nodded, focusing on how his legs had joined hers moving in distorted shapes under the ripples. "Why won't you look at me?"

She turned her face round, opening her eyes comically wide to stare at him. His blond hair was plastered to his scalp, showing ridges left by his fingers where he'd scraped it off his face. It accentuated his broad nose and fleshy cheekbones.

She knew his face so well. There were times when she would be talking to her husband or helping the boys do their homework and she'd have to catch her breath. An image of Patrick would hit her so hard it was as if he was there in the room with her. When she closed her eyes every night, it was Patrick's face she saw next to hers on the pillow. She had imagined every inch so vividly, it was almost disappointing to see him in the flesh.

She shut her eyes briefly now but it was Harry, her eldest son, who floated before her, his dark hair tousled over Thomas the Tank Engine pyjamas, his cheeks red and round with laughter. When she opened her eyes again, it was to find Patrick had put his face close up to hers, almost touching. She hissed at him and he laughed, throwing his head back as if he was putting the line of his neck on display.

The violence of her feelings towards Patrick shocked her. When she thought about her husband it was always with respect, a little distance, but Patrick broke down all her defences. Crossed all her boundaries. She imagined slitting his neck then, a clean cut across the Adam's apple, using the same precision as when she was carving the Sunday roast. The blood would stream out across the surface of the water, rippling over to where the children were playing, interrupting the women gossiping. Most of all it would curl round and round her, trussing her up with strings she couldn't escape from.

"We have to be kind to each other," she said, more fiercely than she meant to. "Otherwise there is no point."

She moved to swim off but he lunged down and grabbed hold of her ankle, tightening his grip so she had to hold on to the side or sink down, unable to kick. He inched his fingers round, moving them individually. It was the same hand action she used with the children. Incy wincy spider. But then Patrick clenched his fist, digging harder and harder into her flesh to push beneath her ankle bone and the rest of her foot. The pain was so unexpected it made her gasp.

"Did you hear about the girl who wakes up one morning and decides she's a masochist?" he asked.

Jane shook her head. She had let go of the side by this time and was trying to look as if she was floating on her back. As if no-one was holding onto her ankle. As if nothing was happening.

"She meets a sadist and everything's fine until he finds a way to really hurt her. Each time she begs for pain, he's nicer and nicer to her, brings her flowers, chocolates, everything. And do you know the thing that really pisses her off? She can't complain to anyone, because they're all so fucking jealous of the way she's met the perfect man."

Patrick pushed Jane off then and she trod water for a few minutes, listening to him laugh. "I love that story," he said. "Causing pain through kindness, and everyone thinking you're some kind of saint."

Jane turned her back on him, and told herself that if she managed to swim to the other end without making one splash, without causing one ripple in the water, then everything would be all right. She didn't even come up for air until she'd reached the half-way mark, and then she took care to emerge very gently.

She swam a few more lengths on her own, trying to fill her mind with thoughts of home. She pictured her children sitting round the kitchen table, Tim reading them stories. It soothed her until she believed she could forget Patrick. By her eighth length, she'd entered the dream zone. She was dimly aware of the other swimmers but it was her body, her place in the water, she was focusing on. All she had to do was to get to the white tiled end, cling on to the silver rail, turn herself round and aim for the other side. The smoochy, late-night music had been turned on now, the over-bright striplights switched off so the building was lit up by spotlights from below the water. Everyone had the same dazed expression. This was the twilight hour and none of them were rushing home.

It was at this hour she'd first met Patrick. She'd swum herself into a trance so when he'd come up beside her, it had been a surprise to look around and see they were alone in the pool. Even the lifeguard had his back to them as he spoke on the poolside telephone. It seemed natural then to swim side by side. They'd nodded to each other a few times before that, exchanging the sort of half smiles you do with someone who shares the same hobby. But that evening changed everything. It was the water that had done it. It suspended reality, encouraging them to talk not about the actualities of their lives but about their dreams.

Later that night, sitting in front of the television beside her husband, she started to shake with the enormity of her betrayal.

"What's wrong?" Tim asked.

What could she say? She often wondered what would have happened if she confessed how a stranger knew that every morning she sat down to breakfast hoping this was going to be the day she would have the courage to run away and leave them all, Tim and the children.

Tim would never have believed her. She was a good mother, a good woman. She wasn't the type to run away. It was Patrick who had seen through her straight away because he had the same unrealistic fantasies. Only his were that he would one day settle down.

"We are so completely opposite," he'd laughed that first time, after they had swum a length in silence taking this in.

"We'd pass each other by in the street without even no-ticing," Jane had agreed. "You are the type of person I would never, ever want to meet." She looked across at him as they swam. "Normally," she added.

But the next Thursday, Jane stood outside the Leisure Centre and paused a second in front of the revolving doors. "If I can get to the other side without having to touch them again, Patrick's going to be inside," she told herself, giving the doors one big push. She'd managed, of course, but then she'd known she would. Jane wasn't the type to play a game of chance unless the odds were heavily stacked in her favour.

Neither Patrick nor Jane had missed a Thursday since.

It hadn't taken them long to find a rhythm to their swimming. They would swim individually at first and then drift together. After a while, they stopped talking and just rested, let-ting their hands trail out with the water's flow towards the other's body before pulling them back. Just in time.

They used to never touch. It had been one of their rules. Jane told herself that it was so she could go home with a clean conscience. A clean mind in a clean body. The water washing everything away. All their dirty secrets carried off by the waves.

Two women in their fifties came up in the medium lane, skirting round Jane. She nodded them on to show she wasn't moving anywhere and they smiled. "Give me some inspiration," Jane overheard one woman say. "What are you feeding him for tea tonight?" She thought of the lasagne she'd got simmering in the oven for Tim and her to share later, but then Patrick kicked his foot out at her calf.

"I'd like to eat off your body," he said. "I'd start at the top. Put canapés over your face. Olives, salami, salty cheeses. I'd have to bite at them, nibble very gently, peck with my lips, and then I'd lick the juices off."

Jane swam off, picking up speed, kicking at the water with her legs. She wondered if she'd put enough tomato sauce in the lasagne, covered it with enough cheese. It would spoil if it dried out. Patrick caught up with her.

"You'd have to lie absolutely still because you'd be the table. Your neck would be covered in the thinnest slices of smoked salmon so I'd need to bend right over you to get hold of one of the ends. I'd have to use my teeth to pull it off, layer by layer. I'd pause a bit then. It would be important to be able to take my time."

"That's hackneyed, trite," Jane said. "A school boy's fantasy." She didn't say what she really felt. That it was the strange innocence of their meetings she had liked. It had been this feeling of talking to a best friend, a mirror image, that had kept her coming back to the pool week after week. Now, she just felt let down by the one-sidedness of the conversation. Patrick had changed their relationship from the shock of shared intimacies to a sordid predictability.

He fell behind her then, tapping the soles of her feet as she swam. She kicked out, splashing wildly until he came back beside her. "There lies the crux," he said. "If you're turned on, there's no point to the game. You mustn't move a muscle otherwise you'll spoil my pleasure."

"And the main course?" she asked. "I suppose you'll put slabs of beef on my breasts and fill my navel with gravy."

They were silent as they turned around for another length, weaving through the other swimmers who were congregating in the shallows. They had found a rhythm now, were matching each other stroke for stroke. Apart from the background music, the pool was unnaturally quiet so Patrick started to whisper.

"I'd turn you round then and eat from your back," he said. "A Chinese banquet, so I could dip in and out as I choose. Fill the hollows made by your shoulder blades, the valleys beside your spine, the dimples just above your buttocks. Nothing too much of anything but just enough to whet my appetite."

She tried hard to feel some frisson of arousal but as she thought about lying there with Patrick bent over her, she started to shudder. In the pictures she was creating in her mind, her hair had turned to seaweed and her legs fell to each side uselessly. If he were to turn her over, her eyes would be gaping holes, her flesh would fall off with each bite. She tried to dismiss the images but a final picture of Patrick licking his lips above her wasted body lingered on.

"Time to go," she said. "I've been in too long."

He nodded and still swimming in unison, they made their way to the metal steps. He moved round to encircle her with his arms as she climbed out in front of him.

'*No Running. No Jumping. No Shouting. No Petting.*'

In front of the notice, a bored lifeguard sat, looking through Jane as if she didn't exist so she shook her wet hair as if by accident and watched the drops of water land on his bare sunbed-tanned thighs. He brushed them off still without reacting, semi-focusing on a spot in the distance.

"Pudding from your legs." Patrick was whispering behind Jane as they walked towards the Jacuzzi. "Custard to suck from between your toes, jelly up and down your legs and ..."

She turned round and put her hand over his mouth as the two women from the pool shuffled round the Jacuzzi bench to make room for them. Jane and Patrick sat there in silence, legs and hands entwined under the cover of the bubbles, heads resting back on the ledge.

After a while, the women resumed their conversation. "No, swimming's the thing," one said. She was wearing a pink and orange flowered swimming hat which clashed with the red flush on her neck and cheeks. Jane closed her eyes. "I've tried all sorts of exercise but when you get older, you've got to be careful, haven't you?"

"I tried jogging once," volunteered the other woman. Patrick made running movements with his fingers along the inside of Jane's thigh. She squeezed her legs together to catch his hand, knowing he wouldn't try to free himself.

"Never again," said the woman. "I couldn't walk properly for days. It turned my legs to jelly. Jelly and custard they were."

Jane gasped, and when she turned to look at Patrick, he'd ducked his head under the water. Jane passed her hand several times over where he'd been as if she was showing off a magician's trick. The Disappearing Man. When he surfaced, she pushed him gently down again, holding her palm flat on top of his hair.

Later, Jane lay in bed with her legs drawn up to her stomach, her back to Tim. He tapped her on the shoulder but she shrugged him off, pretending to be half-asleep. She could feel him kiss her back gently, his tongue grazing her skin, but then he stopped, rolling away to the other side of the bed.

"You taste different," he said. "What is it?"

She lay there, not breathing, holding her arm up in front of her to see if her hand was shaking. Slowly, she moved it to her lips and licked it tentatively. Then she laughed.

"It's just the chlorine," she said. "I didn't have time for a shower."

"I like it." He shifted onto his side so the bed creaked. "It reminds me of those American swimmers, all shoulders and smiles."

She turned to face him and took his face in between her palms, studying it hard. "You," she said seriously, "are my an-

chor in life. You tie me down. Without you, I'd float away."
Then she gave him her version of a wide American smile.

"You're always happy these days," he said, as if he was
accusing her of something.

She was happy. The thought surprised her. She pushed
both - the thought and her surprise at it - to the back of her
mind to consider later.

"I'll have to come swimming with you." His fingers were
playing with the hair that curled at the back of her neck. He was
always touching her, playing with her. "If it's so much fun," he
added.

She flopped down on her back and sighed. "I'm not
going again," she said. "It doesn't do me any good. I think it
must be all the chemicals they put in the water."

"But..."

She interrupted him then, reaching out to stop him saying anything else. But as they moved back across the bed towards each other, she tried not to notice how clumsy their
movements were, swimming on land.

Blind

I wonder if he will want to stroke my face. I've seen it on the films. The celluloid blind man stretches across while the girl, always beautiful, closes her eyes and gives herself up to his touch.

I'm not beautiful but that morning I dress carefully. Phil watches as I preen in front of the mirror. His expression - half-cynical, half-amused - shows he knows it's not for him.

"I've heard women are gagging to do it with blind men," he says. "Lucky buggers."

"Hardly the description I'd use." I smooth my skirt down in the front with both hands. I'm a home-help so I normally wear tracksuits during the day. Wearing a skirt makes me feel different. Less eager to please.

Phil lurches towards me, his eyes tightly shut, hands outstretched. "Fancy me, do you?" he says. "Want me to touch you all over?"

I push past him out the door. "I'm late," I say.

Phil is going to leave me. On the way to meet my new blind client, I sit on a park bench and when I touch up my make-up, the reflection in the mirror tells me what I've known for a long time inside.

Maybe Phil will still be there when I come back. Maybe not. I try to care but when nothing happens, I check my handbag to make sure I've got the right address and take one last look in the mirror to see whether I've got lipstick on my teeth.

"You're one hard woman," I tell myself and as I walk down the street, my skirt tight on my hips, I imagine high heels clicking. For those few hundred steps, I'm really someone.

It's so hot in the blind man's front room I have to pinch myself to stop my eyes closing. Robert Evans and I are sitting opposite each other on brown floral armchairs. Robert's face is fixed towards the wall, his neck so erect that I take in his profile like a painting. Even when he talks, he has none of the animation I'm used to, and I'm aware that I'm stiller too. A one-sided mirror.

We have nothing to say. It's just a courtesy call, this first visit. I'm not supposed to start cleaning straight away because, according to the agency, we need to get to know and trust each other, but Robert isn't like my normal clients. It's the company most of them are after. I can be the only person they speak to all day, but during the half hour I've been with Robert the phone has gone continuously. While he talks to Ian or Glen or Sam, I look round the room carefully, telling myself I'm checking out Robert's flat for professional reasons.

"That's almost an antique," he says suddenly. "Press that little lever on the side, put a coin on his tongue and watch his eyes roll in thanks."

I put the tin money box back down quickly, the thick red lips and round staring eyes turned away to the wall, and scan Robert's face. "How did you know...?" I stop. Why do I feel guilty?

"It's the first thing everyone picks up," he says. "They wouldn't do it if I could see them, but it's only a joke. After all, if something's funny, how can it be wrong?"

I nod, and then remember, saying yes louder than I mean to so I almost shout it out. The phone rings again and

Robert answers. I don't move this time, my hands like fists at my sides, as I listen to Robert make an appointment to meet someone later that night.

"Must go now," I hear him say. He can't know how close I'm standing to him. "I've someone with me. My new girl from Hands-On-Help. Oh, but do listen. She's called Elsie. Such an upstairs, downstairs name, darling."

I go on top of Phil that night, but not before I shut his eyes as carefully as if I'm laying out a corpse. Every time he tries to open them, I press them shut with my palms until he gives up and twists his head from side to side as I ride him, his mouth searching unseeingly for mine. I don't come but he's so surprised at my initiative, he doesn't notice this.

Afterwards we lie side by side, fingers entwined.

"I could have made more of myself," I say, staring at the watermark on the ceiling we've never got round to painting out. "I wasn't thick at school, just bored. It wasn't my fault."

Phil is silent. He's heard all this before.

"I'm going to try that Open University. Get some qualifications. Get out of here. You could do it too," I say. "We're clever, Phil. I'm tired of all these people thinking they're better than us."

I look at Phil but he's fallen asleep, smiling.

"It's not fucking funny," I tell him, but he doesn't wake up.

The next morning I'm still cross so I shout at Phil when he talks about my blind man at breakfast.

"He's not mine," I say. "He's just a client. Like Mrs Robinson."

Phil pauses from spooning cereal into his mouth to snort. He'd come with me last week to help Mrs Robinson with her garden and she made a big fuss about inviting him into the kitchen to have his tea.

"Times have changed, dear," she shouted across Phil at me as if he wasn't there. She was just like a little bird, tip-tapping around the place in tiny patent shoes, prodding at things with sharp painted nails. All the make-up she put on - blue eye-shadow, red lipstick, nail varnish - sat on her leathery skin like enamel paint on black crow feathers. Normally I love the way she pretends we are both aristocrats temporarily down on our luck, but while the game is fun when we're on our own, with Phil there her flutey vowels drill into me. "You have to consort with the help nowadays," she lowered her voice semi-confidentially. "Still, it's sweet how grateful they are."

I didn't look at Phil, although later on when he was back in the garden, I watched him from the upstairs window. He was kneeling at the edge of the flower bed carefully plucking out the few pansy seedlings Mrs Robinson had managed to plant by herself.

I want to ask him about it now, but I know he will pre-tend it was a mistake and I don't want him to lie to me.

"I don't think he's very nice," I say instead. "The blind man."

I ring Penny at the Hands-On-Help agency and tell her I will accept Robert Evans. Putting it like that makes me feel better, but she just grunts distractedly.

"You don't know anything about a silver bowl Mrs Rob-inson's lost, do you Else?" she asks. "She keeps ringing us up about it. Silly old cow's probably put it in a cupboard some-where and forgotten about it. I swear she gets dottier every day."

I know the bowl. I bloody well should as Mrs Robinson gets me to polish it every week. It used to sit in the hall of her home for visitors to leave their calling cards in when she was a child. "Did you have one like that, Elsa?" she'd asked me the first time she showed it to me. "Didn't it used to be lovely when people came calling?" But I don't tell Penny any of this. She's often put in these difficult positions between the client and us, her girls as she likes to call us, and I appreciate the fact that she isn't telling me about how Mrs Robinson has accused me of stealing.

"Elsa," Penny sounds hesitant, "you didn't take a friend round to Mrs Robinson's, did you? It's only she's banging on about some weirdo who picked all her flowers."

I burst out laughing, thinking how Phil would react if he heard Mrs Robinson call him a weirdo. "Yes," I say calmly, "I invited all my mates round for a party. It's what I always do with clients. Frolicking in the flower bed is just the half of it. And I've got that silver dish stacked away with all the other goodies I've nicked."

"I know, I know, but no harm in asking." I can hear the scratch of her pen as she marks my days for doing Robert Evans on this big Year Planner she's got fixed to the wall above her desk.

I dream that Mrs Robinson and Robert Evans are dancing the polka while I clean round them. Mrs Robinson is wearing pink stiletto heels that pierce through the hose of my vacuum cleaner and suddenly dust shoots out of the gash she has made in the rubber. It covers Mrs Robinson like confetti, turning her white hair black so she looks younger, her bright red lipstick jaunty and less ridiculous. With each step she looks more and more like me while Robert dances on impervious. His dead eyes fixed on mine over her shoulder.

Robert says I mustn't mind if he shouts at me. "It's my nature, Elsie," he says. "I have to let things out," and he touches the skin on my arm very lightly.

"Elsie," he says then. Just that, Elsie, and although I wait, he says nothing else. We stand there together like we are about to dance, and I want to cry so badly that I'm shaking and can't tell him my name's Elsa, not Elsie.

Another day, I'm dusting the ornaments on his mantelpiece when I get the sudden urge to look at him. He's sitting there, hands on his knees, and it's as if he's waiting for something. Then the phone rings and he reaches out and picks it up without any change of expression. His voice is so loud, I guess he's never learnt to worry about the impact he had on anyone else. He has lots of friends, Robert, and he talks to them like he's a girl in some black and white Sunday afternoon film. "Darling," I overhear him say one day. "I care so terribly about what will happen to you." I try to imagine Phil saying something like this, but it's impossible.

I tell Mrs Robinson about Robert although it's one of Penny's golden rules that we're never to discuss clients with other clients. I think it's nerves that makes me do it. Mrs Robinson has taken to following me round from room to room, watching my every move. We are no longer a team. When she talks to me her voice is everyday, ordinary and she doesn't tell me any of her stories about what it is like to grow up rich. The silence, and her looking, make me talk more.

"I can't imagine what it must be like to be blind," I say. "How would you know about colours, for example? If you were blind, Mrs Robinson, I could tell you that the sun was the same colour as the grass and you'd believe me, wouldn't you?"

"But then if I couldn't see them, it wouldn't make much difference. Careful!" She takes a glass decanter off the edge of the cupboard, cradling it in her arms as if she has rescued it from a certain splintering fall. I want to tell her that I have never broken anything of hers yet, but I haven't finished with Robert.

"And he has all these things," I say. "All these ornaments. Why does he have those? They're all arranged just so. He notices if I've moved anything and tells me off the next time."

"At least he's still got them," Mrs Robinson says. "I should ring Penny up so she can warn him to look out."

"Look out. That's a good one," I laugh but then I get her real meaning and we say nothing else to each other all morning.

It was only going to happen the once. I still don't know what made me do it the first time. It must be the same impulse to push to the edge that you get when you're standing on a river-bank or top of high mountain. You know, to throw your keys over so you've lost your home, your car, sealed the lock on every door that lets you through to safety. Either that or it's Phil going on about how all women found blind men sexy. Personally, I don't but maybe for once I just want to be like all those other women, so one morning when, as usual, Robert is on the phone to one of his friends, I take off all my clothes and just stand there. Naked. Then I pick up the vacuum cleaner, and start hoovering around Robert's chair.

"No, no, no," he says, "you always soak the strawberries in vodka first. Elsie, stop it. I'm talking." He carries on his phone conversation without a break so I don't understand at first. Then I turn off the vacuum cleaner and stand close to where he's sitting. Where he always sat. The wool fibres of his jumper are only centimetres away from my bare breasts.

"That's better," he says, and I run my hands up and down my body, my fingers moving between my legs as I listen to him talk. His face is fixed on the space between my left nipple and my navel. I roll my head from side to side, my tongue hanging out in a pantomime copy of a porn star reaching climax. Then, as Robert gossips to his friend about dinner parties and recipes, I wave my sticky fingers under his nose. I swear I see him flinch.

"If it feels good, I say just do it," he says into the phone and then he laughs like a hyena. Screech, screech.

"I'll see you in two days time, Robert," I call out as I stand at the front door, buttoning up my coat against the cold.

"That was Elsie. Oh, she's so hopeless I can't tell you." I hear him complaining as I shut the door.

Now, every time I go to Robert's, I take off my clothes and leave them in a neat pile by the bookcase. I've got to like cleaning in the nude, feeling my breasts swing as I dust and scrub, hearing the slight whoosh as my bare buttocks hit Robert's sofa when I take my tea break.

Even Phil's noticed there's something different about me.

"It's not that I'm complaining," he tells me as we lie together after having sex one weekday afternoon. "It's just a bit surprising, that's all. You never used to like it."

I think about this. In my head, I've always liked sex. It's just turning it into a reality that's been the problem. I've never been one of these people who can separate the two. Think about someone while making love to someone else. I need to be there, present and correct in the act.

"I just want you," I say. And then I smile, because it's true and I'm not sure why, but I do know it feels good.

I'm cleaning in the nude at Robert's one Wednesday when the phone rings. I wait for Robert to pick it up but he doesn't. Just sits there, letting it ring. Eventually I can't bear it anymore.

"Will I get that?" I say, reaching out to pick up the receiver.

"Leave it, Elsie," he says, and I have no idea whether it is just instinct that makes him lean across and touch me because he can't have known I'm there. His fingers land on my rib cage, flutter there and then move up, scraping my breast until they press my nipple. I shut my eyes instinctively, and when I open them again, his hand is resting palm up on his knee, his finger tips curl inwards to make a bowl. "Just leave it," he repeats.

"But.."

The phone stops ringing.

"Robert," I start. If he'd only show some reaction. "I'll get on then," I say, and I don't know why I'm crying so hard as I pick up my clothes and take them out into the hall to dress.

I phone Penny that evening. I've been on edge all day, expecting her to ring me to say that Robert has called her but she just says: "Hi Else, what's new?" Suddenly, I realise I've nothing to say.

"I don't want to go to Mrs Robinson any more," I say at last. "She makes me feel like a thief. I can't bear it."

"Oh Elsa." Penny sounds so tired sometimes I wonder how she can stand it. Cleaning is more than a job to her, of course. It really is a vocation. That's why she specialises in the sort of clients no one else will touch. She wants them to have nice and tidy houses in the same way other people want to save their souls.

"She's just old," Penny says. "You used to get on so well. Do you want me to talk to her?"

"Pen'll fix it," Phil says as he watches me put down the receiver. He's lying on the bed, shirt unbuttoned, his fly open. He has even got one eye shut, as if he's tottering on the brink of something, half of him already gone. Both Phil and I are sex-sated these days. We're living in one of those states of fever when it seems a waste of effort to get dressed properly. It will only be a matter of time before we have to take everything off.

"Come here," he leers, but I shake him off. I can't stop thinking about Robert's hand touching my breast. It was creepy, like the hand of a dead person. Why hasn't he said anything?

I'm not taking any chances with Mrs Robinson, so the next day I turn up with a box of pansies and ring the front door bell instead of going straight in by the side as normal.

She raises one eyebrow when she saw me standing there. "My, my," she says and folded her arms in front of her. "It's like a beau come courting."

I smile and hold them out to her but she doesn't take them. "They look a bit dirty," she says.

"Mrs Robinson..."

152

"Yes, little Miss Elsa? Don't you go trying to butter me up. I let you into my house, Elsa, but you let me down. I can see straight through you and your sort."

I burst into tears right there and then on the doorstep. "I'm sorry," I say, making to brush my face with my jacket sleeve, the pansies swaying in front of my eyes. I sniff into the wool. "I just want us to be like we were."

"What were we ever really like?" she asks. "You put that bowl back on the doorstep tonight, Elsa, and we'll say no more about it."

"I haven't got ..."

Mrs Robinson turns then and shuts the door on me. I wait for a moment but when nothing happens, I bend down and leave the pansies on the step, their little faces peering over the frilly edge of the box like kittens looking for a home.

When Phil comes back from work that evening, I'm sitting on the edge of the bed waiting for him. He's already unzipping his trousers as he walks through the door and when he sees me, he smiles.

"Well, that's the kind of welcome I like," he says, and he comes to sit next to me, pulling my naked body close against his.

I hand him the box I've been holding without speaking and he kisses my shoulder, letting his tongue trail along the skin, before he looks at it.

"What's this?" he asks, and then, as he starts picking out objects from the box, he repeats the question but this time with different emphasis. "What *is* this?"

I pick up the stupid money box and pull the lever, showing him how the eyes roll and tongue sticks out as the gaudily painted face begs for scraps. Phil shakes his head and picks up a book of poetry.

"You don't even read poetry," he says, flicking through the pages without looking at them.

"I could have done," I reply. "It's not my fault I've never been taught properly."

"And this is Mrs Robinson's bowl," he ignores me and starts laying the contents of the box out on to the bed in lines. "We'll have to call Penny."

"They are just things," I say, looking at the objects with tired eyes. There seem so many of them when they are laid out like that. "If things had been different, they could have been mine."

"They're still other people's things," Phil says.

"We're worth more than any of this, Phil." Then I fall to my knees at his feet and hold on his jumper, pinching the edge of it between my fingers.

"Get up, Elsa," he says. "Go and get some clothes on."

Phil says he wants some time to think.

"About what?" I scream.

"You really don't get it, do you?" he says.

I don't. "It's your fault,' I say. 'You never talk to me. Haven't we been fine. Hasn't the sex been fine?"

"Yes but." He takes so long to speak, I want to shake him. "Even that seems stolen now, Elsa. You're living in a fantasy."

It makes me cry when I see how little the bag is that Phil packs all his stuff in. I spend the first night on my own searching the flat for something of his, something I can smell or touch or taste. Nothing. He's picked our home dry of him.

Penny gives me time off to recover, but two weeks later I ring her up to tell her I've got a place at University. I won't be cleaning for her any more. She's surprised but pleased for me.

"I don't know what I'm going to do without you," she says. "All your clients will miss you so much."

"And I'll miss them," I'm not sure if this is a lie, or not.

Penny sucks in her breath, and starts that wheedling tone I've heard so many times before when she wants me to do something she knows I won't like.

"I know I shouldn't ask you but do you think, that just this time, you could, as a personal favour..."

"Penny, just ask me straight. If it's something I can do, I will."

I stand at Robert's door and breathe heavily before I turn the key.

"It's just me," I shout and lean up against the hall wall as I wait for him to reply. When I hear nothing, I shout again. "Penny asked me to come today and clean up for you because you're having a party tonight. You asked her especially for extra help but I was the only one that was available. I'm leaving the agency actually. Going to University." After a few more lines of this, I tell myself to shut up and busy myself with putting away my jacket and changing my shoes into the soft soled ones I use for cleaning.

When I turn round, Robert is standing in the doorway, his eyes fixed on the spot behind me.

"Hello," I say. "Haven't seen you in a long time."

"Nor I you," he says, and then smiles. His face looks so different like that, I can't stop staring. Normally, the small lines around his mouth give him a pursed look, as if he's disapproving of what he can't see.

"Is your party anything special tonight?" I ask, circling round him to get at the hoover and cleaning materials so I don't have to touch him.

"My cleaning lady is going to university?" he says, making it sound like a question. Why doesn't he go and sit down?

I clean the dining room first, polishing the table so that I can see my reflection in the wood and when I go back into the hall, Robert is still there. It is the longest I have ever been in the flat without the phone ringing and when I look at it, I notice that the receiver was off. As soon as I replace the handset, it starts ringing. I pick it up, put it in Robert's hand without saying anything and start to lug the hoover up stairs.

Two hours later, I go through to the sitting room. Robert is sitting in his chair, headphones on, his hand tapping on the arm of his chair in time to the music he's listening to. I touch his shoulder lightly to get his attention.

"I'm going," I say. It seems odd not to shake hands or anything, but Robert makes no movement apart from taking off his headphones.

Then he raises his hand up and leaves it hanging in the air, trembling slightly. I move a few inches, twisting my body so the material from my cotton sweatshirt brushes against his fingers. He nods and shuts his eyes.

"Have a lovely evening," I call out as I shut the door behind me, checking my pocket again to make sure I've left his keys behind. That I've taken nothing of his with me.

I run all the way up the street, the high heels I'm still not used to click clacking under me, my knees knocking as my shins knife up behind and I try to find a new balance. Then as if I'd conjured him up out of my need, Phil steps out of a dark alley and catches me just as I'm about to give up. We both laugh as I throw my whole weight into his arms.

"Penny rang me," he says. "Told me about you leaving her. She wanted to hear all about it. Kept saying how well you'd done getting into university like that. Oh, Elsa."

I think of how I've left Robert sitting alone in that chair, and for a moment I felt guilty.

"Me," I say. "I'm nothing."

But when we walk off, I notice that Phil and I are in step, our arms linked to make a human wall in the street, not letting anyone past. For those few moments, I really am someone.